EUROPIA

EUROPIA

Anthony Etherington

The Book Guild Ltd

First published in Great Britain in 2022 by
The Book Guild
Unit E2, Airfield Business Park
Harrison Road
Market Harborough
Leicestershire, LE16 7UL
Freephone: 0800 999 2982
www.bookguild.co.uk
Email: info@bookguild.co.uk
Twitter: @bookguild

Typeset in 11pt Minion Pro

Printed and bound in the UK by TJ Books LTD, Padstow, Cornwall

ISBN 978 1914471 254

British Library Cataloguing in Publication Data.
A catalogue record for this book is available from the British Library.

For Robbie

ONE

Marta tightened her dressing-gown cord and padded across the kitchen to release the window blind.

'How about that, boy?' she cried as sunlight flooded the tiny space. 'Spring at last.'

Gypsy jumped off the sofa and trotted over to weave himself around his owner's calves. Having delivered a brisk good-morning stroke, Marta flicked on the radio, opened a can of cat food and started spooning chunks into Gypsy's dish.

'...The recent surge in people-smuggling has seen security at ports and rail hubs tightened,' the newsreader reported. 'Meanwhile, police have widened the search for club hostess Ludmilla Fedoruk—'

'Gypsy, shush.'

Marta stopped what she was doing and turned up the volume.

'...last seen on Thursday at a restaurant in downtown Caradea.'

Marta let out a sigh and set the dish down on its mat. She was about to reach for the scoop to tackle Gypsy's litter tray when her palmcom started buzzing. She rarely welcomed early morning calls; usually it was her mother with some new complaint or David Brisco, her section head, requesting a shift change. Marta checked the caller ID, summoned a smile and pressed 'RECEIVE'.

A wizened old woman appeared on the screen, cigarette between her lips, a gnarled hand clutching her blouse.

'Hi, Mama.'

'Can you get me some more books today, dear?'

'Good morning, darling daughter, what a lovely—'

Mrs Ionescu coughed vigorously and lurched forward, filling the screen with a close-up of her white, wiry hair.

'And don't get me any more Fischer,' she gasped. 'Church Council meetings are more exciting than his pap.'

Marta suppressed a smile. In recent years her mother had developed a voracious appetite for crime and trashy love stories, the sort of books she would have burned if she'd ever found them in her kids' possession. That said, she could still recite whole verses of poetry and the scriptures, and often did Sundays after lunch.

'OK, I'll drop by on my way home.'

'I thought you were off today?'

'No, Mama. I told you yesterday, I swapped shifts.'

'…Traffic on the south circular is at a standstill.'

'You hear that, girl, you're going to be late.'

Marta glanced at the clock on the cooker.

'Jesus, I'm due at Union House at nine!'

'Marta Alina, don't you dare take our Saviour's name in vain!'

'Sorry, Mama, I'll call you later. Bye.'

Marta tapped her palmcom and dashed through to the bathroom.

Five minutes later, dressed in a smart patterned blouse and crimson cruise pants, Marta hurriedly packed her satchel – swimming gear, lunchbox, tablet – and pulled on her denim jacket. Crossing to the front door she lifted the StunMaster personal defence device from its charger and slipped it into her bag.

'Bye, Gypsy,' she said, checking that the cat was in his basket as she unlocked the front door. 'See you tonight.'

Stepping out onto the walkway, Marta double-locked the door and headed for the stairwell.

*

Emerging into dazzling sunshine, Marta pulled on her sunglasses and strode briskly down the footpath, savouring the warmth of the sun on her back. Judging by the number of open windows in the dreary low-rise blocks, the balconies festooned with washing, her neighbours, too, were appreciating the change in weather. Out on Meresti, the broad avenue bisecting the sprawling Goval estate, ageing buses rumbled up the hill and battered taxis jostled for business. People were smiling; even the taxi drivers' curses sounded good-natured.

Further on Marta came across Ion Gheorghiu sitting in his kiosk reading his newspaper, unfazed as ever by the blast of horns and buzzers barely a metre from his back. When he glanced up and saw Marta approaching, Ion grinned and stroked his thick grey moustache.

'Did you watch the match, Marta, did you see my boy?'

Ion's son Paolo was a regular at the youth club Marta ran on Friday evenings at St Vincent's. The lad was a great favourite – tall, lean and handsome – and a talented footballer who had represented his college in Wednesday's regional youth finals. Although no great fan of the sport, Marta had been thrilled to see the youngster's winning goal replayed on the regional news.

'Yeah, he was a real star, Ion. Listen, we're going to put on a little celebration for him Friday night. Tell Angela not to breathe a word, OK?'

'God bless you, Marta,' Gheorghiu senior said, beaming. 'We'll be there... He's my pride, you know. And my pension.'

Marta laughed and waved Ion goodbye; how often had she heard that line before! Less than a minute later she arrived at the bus stop and joined the lengthy queue behind two giggling schoolgirls in summer uniform. Listening to the kids chatter on excitedly about a recent school dance, the cute boys and furtive fumblings, Marta closed her eyes and tilted her face towards the sun. God, how she used to loathe those hideous Saturday-night socials in the village hall at Rietsa, being chatted up and fretting about rejection while her mother kept a permanent weather eye out for prospective husbands. Unlike these two, there was no way she would ever have dared ask a boy for a dance. She admired their spirit though. *What must it be like to watch your own flesh and blood grow, to love someone not because of their looks or wit or success, but simply because of who they are?* It was not too late to find out, of course, although, given her track record with men, the odds were not great, especially now that Arpad seemed to be going off the boil. Perhaps she should just forget the whole idea, settle for a comfortable, selfish existence. She had her friends and Gypsy, a good job and her books—

A fast-approaching siren brought Marta's musing to an abrupt end. Opening her eyes she saw a lime-chequered squad car tear down the middle of the road, blue lights flashing. Close behind a drone followed at rooftop level, its low hum sending vibrations through her ribcage and setting off every dog in the vicinity. Almost unnoticed, the bus arrived from the opposite direction and lurched to a halt, panels rattling, brakes hissing. The doors opened with a tired wheeze and the queue shuffled forward. As Marta stepped aboard and swiped her palmcom over the auto-toll, the young transport cop sitting behind the driver ran his eyes over her. She smiled and felt a flutter in her chest. Since passing thirty she had come to appreciate a bit of recognition.

*

Hurrying along King Michael Avenue in downtown Caradea, Marta felt a surge of pride as she caught sight of Union House up ahead gleaming in the sunshine, the building's neo-classical cornices and pediments silhouetted against its white plaster façade. VisionPlace, her employers, had recently invested millions in a complete refurbishment of the late nineteenth-century town house and it showed. Reopened just seven months ago, it now housed the offices of the Regional Commission (Eastern Region) of the UES, the Union of European States. Since then, Marta, a member of the project team that had overseen the refurbishment, had met every Thursday with her opposite number in the secretariat, Claudia Lacroix, to identify and address any problems with the building's ongoing maintenance. The two women had developed a close and effective working relationship and Marta had come to look forward to their meetings.

As usual that morning, Marta and Claudia sat at the round meeting table next to the window in Claudia's office overlooking the river. The Facilities Manager was in a buoyant mood.

'So, all items are in hand and I have *no* new matters to raise,' she said with a confirmatory smile. 'Coffee?'

'Hallelujah! I think that's the least we deserve,' Marta replied.

Claudia got up and crossed to the fancy coffee machine on the sideboard.

'I hope you don't think we've been unreasonable,' she said, adjusting the settings on the machine.

'No, I didn't mean… I'm just disappointed that there have been so many niggly bits 'n' bobs since you moved in.'

A hiss, a gurgle and the job was done.

'True. But you're always on the case tout de suite, Marta. I know I can rely on you one hundred per cent.'

Claudia returned with the coffees and sat back down.

'Besides, today marks a turning point. Another week or two with low or zero defects and we can make these meetings fortnightly or even monthly.'

Marta nodded sportingly and sipped her coffee but inside

she was torn. Reducing the frequency of their trouble-shooting meetings would be seen as a mark of improvement by Claudia's bosses and David. However, she had come to treasure her end-of-meeting chats with the personable, if forthright, Frenchwoman, especially since discovering that Claudia was a former international water polo player.

'I broke my PB on Tuesday,' Marta said, making no attempt to hide her pride. 'The eight hundred.'

Claudia's face lit up.

'Breaststroke?'

'Freestyle.'

'Oh, well done you!' she cried. 'So what will you be aiming—'

A tap was followed by a vexed-looking woman sticking her head around the door.

'I'm sorry to interrupt, Claudia, but I wondered, while you have Ms Ionescu here, if I might have a word?'

'Of course, come in,' Claudia said, a confident smile on her face. 'Whatever the problem, Marta will fix it.'

Turning to Marta, she added, 'Janine works in Accounts, Marta.'

'Hi, Janine,' Marta said, suspecting that her UES colleague had just dropped her in the proverbial.

The woman grimaced and bustled into the room, the aggravation on her face seeming to grow the closer to Marta she came.

'It's about the rent, Ms Ionescu. VisionPlace took an additional payment in March.'

'I see. It's not something... Have you raised this with your Accounts contact?'

'No. I only discovered the overpayment this morning.'

'OK. May I suggest that—'

'They're so unreliable. I leave messages and they don't call back, I g-mail and they don't reply.'

Janine went on like this for what felt like an age, rejecting Marta's suggestions, dissing her VisionPlace colleagues. Marta remained calm but was fuming inside: whatever the rights of her complaint, Janine's manner was offensive and unhelpful. In the end, after promising that she would pursue the matter with her Accounts colleagues, Marta left, glad to have escaped.

The short walk to Central Terminus gave her the chance to calm down. Thankfully, she had missed the morning rush hour and the terminus was considerably quieter than it usually was when she passed through first thing. Finding plenty of seats on the tram out to Jacquira, the leafy business park where she worked, she sat down next to a young woman wearing headphones, took out her tablet and started on her latest download, a Jack Olaru whodunnit. Unfortunately, repeated messages from her friend and VisionPlace colleague Dina Constantinescu – 'Where are you? When will you be back?' – interrupted Marta's attempts to kick-start her morning, while the non-stop adverts playing on the vehicle's screens sounded even louder than usual, proving a further distraction. By the time she stepped down outside VisionPlace's sprawling, ultra-modern HQ, some twenty minutes later, Marta was out of sorts with herself and everybody else.

TWO

Entering the Sector 11 Property Services Bureau, Marta marched past the rows of agents in their bays typing or talking on the phone and headed straight for David's glass-walled office. Tapping briskly on the door she entered the forensically tidy space – a shrine to order and efficiency – and plonked herself down in front of the desk where her boss was sitting, his eyes glued to the screen. At length, David looked up.

'Good meeting?'

'Great, until I was ambushed by some tartar from Accounts. I told her she needed to speak to her contact but she wouldn't have it.'

'Do you know who she was?'

'Just some departmental minion got her knickers in a twist.'

David frowned.

'Been studying the Customer Focus handbook, have we?'

'I know, I know, but it drives me mad. We give them extensive contact lists, direct access to their account managers, and still they bleat like infants. It's pathetic.'

'So what was the problem?'

'She reckoned they've been overcharged on their rent,

something about incomplete quarters. I asked if she'd spoken to Accounts and she—'

'What are you going to do?'

'I'm going to speak to Jane Horowitz.'

'Good. So what do you want from me?'

'She said it's the second quarter in a row this has happened. I thought you could raise it with the management team, mistakes like this are bad for our PR.'

David's attention was already waning, his eyes flicking towards his screen.

'OK. So when you've spoken to Jane let me know what she says—'

'And you'll take—'

'And I'll consider taking it to the management team.'

'Good. I thought—'

David resumed his keyboard tapping.

'Thanks, Marta. Leave it with me.'

Marta grunted, got to her feet and headed for the door.

'By the way,' David called after her, grinning, 'residential's got a backlog of repair assessments so I've said we'll help them out. I've forwarded one to you, in Petreni. It's urgent.'

Marta smiled, cheered by the news.

'Petreni? Thanks, boss.'

'I thought that would put a smile on your face.'

Marta did indeed smile as she exited the office. Another trip out. Happy days!

*

Approaching her bay, Marta could see Dina, her buxom and flirtatious neighbour, pouting exaggeratedly. Marta groaned and put down her satchel.

'So what's with the sourpuss?'

Dina slipped down her headset and nodded at David's office.

'Brown-nose Billy was after you and your diary was empty. Again! You didn't answer my messages neither.'

'Fool. He knew I was going to the Union House Facilities meeting.'

'"*The Union House Facilities meeting*",' Dina sneered.

Marta took off her jacket and hung it over the end of the partition then reached down to switch on her terminal. The triumphant opening bars of the VisionPlace anthem provided the perfect intro for her news.

'He's given me an assessment to do. In Petreni.'

'Petreni! You jammy bitch. How come you get Petreni and I get the scrag ends?'

Marta savoured any opportunity to wind up her friend. She lifted her hand and crossed her fingers.

'Me and Dave, just like that.'

The incoming call indicator on Dina's headset flashed.

'Well, just keep your sodding diary up to date, hon, for Christ's sake. Pretty please.'

Dina pulled on her headset.

'VisionPlace Property Services, Dina speaking. How may I help you?'

*

Marta swore under her breath. Her keyboard had frozen and a familiar message was flashing on the screen.

> *'You have exceeded the maximum permitted exposure period and your terminal has been disconnected. Why not visit one of the staff relaxation facilities or take a walk outside? If you choose the latter, make sure to protect yourself against the sun. Your terminal will be reconnected in fifteen minutes.'*

Leaning back in her chair, Marta yawned and stretched her arms. Across the top of her monitor she could see Dina's grinning face.

'You been kicked off again? You'll be getting a visit if you don't watch out.'

Marta shrugged her shoulders and sighed. She hated month-end, the mind-numbing hours spent inputting claims for federal funding.

'Huh! Beats me how they expect us to finish these pain-in-the-arse returns when we keep getting shut down every few minutes.'

'Don't exaggerate,' Dina chided, before mimicking the grotesquely sincere voiceover in the corporate health and safety video: '"You *know* how important your wellbeing is to us."'

'Creeps. They'll be wanting to inspect our shit next.'

Dina paused to flutter her eyelashes at a passing male.

'Strikes me you could do with a visit from the Productivity Team, girl. That nice young Nicholae can work on my finger technique any time.'

Marta rolled her eyes.

'You're so disgusting.'

Dina blew her colleague a kiss.

'Girl can't help her nature.'

With a shake of her head, Marta reached down for her satchel.

'I'm going for a swim.'

*

The fine weather had lured a great many employees outside for lunch and, on exiting the changing rooms, Marta found, much to her satisfaction, that the pool was practically empty. Clad in her black racer swimsuit she crossed to the edge and executed a near-perfect dive, gliding a full half-length underwater before breaking into a breaststroke, her head surging above the water. Back and forth she went, length after length, alternating between breaststroke and front crawl, displaying surprising strength and endurance for one so short and wiry. On completing the session, Marta grabbed hold of the finger grip and jabbed her watch. Seeing her time she waved her fist in the air, delighted.

Later, her damp black hair glistening in the sunshine, she exited the rear of the building and followed the path that led around the wetlands, relishing the sound of the ducks courting and squabbling out on the water. Every seat she passed was in use and the grass was still damp after the past week's prolonged downpours so Marta carried on to the picnic area at the far side of the site. There she approached a group of women from Data Processing sitting at the largest bench table.

'Hi, girls. Room for a skinny'un?'

'Ugh, it's Yokel!'

Minna Matache was a spiteful bitch, the only person in the whole of VisionPlace who still thought it clever, thirteen years after Marta and her family had moved to Caradea, to make jokes about her rural upbringing.

'Come sniffing for leftovers, eh, Marta?'

'You won't find any here, ha ha.'

Marta eyed the women's fleshy arms and plump thighs.

'I can see that!' she said.

'Huh. No wonder you have so much trouble with men,' Minna sneered. 'They like a bit of something to get hold of. Who wants to sleep with a bag of bones?'

A wave of coarse laughter swept over the group. But Marta had learned how to handle Matache and her type in the army: stay cool and ignore their puerile jibes. It just got them more riled! Unfazed, she marched up to the youngster on the end of the line.

'Shift up, Clara.'

The women muttered as they shuffled along to make space.

'So, what news from the number crunchers?'

Minna scowled.

'I don't suppose month-end means much to you shit-hot front liners.'

Clara murmured in Marta's ear.

'Rumours of federal budget cuts. Frankfurt wants us on stand-by from 1.00.'

Marta nodded thoughtfully and retrieved her lunchbox from her bag. Minna grunted, crunched up her orange polystyrene container and tossed it into the nearby waste bin.

'Five minutes, ladies, shift your butts. Let's leave Marta to enjoy her parsley sprigs and vinaigrette in peace.'

Five containers were noisily crunched up and thrown towards the bin. One of them missed, spilling chunks of reconstituted chicken and greasy fries onto the path.

'Fucking hell, Sofia,' Minna sneered. 'Are you crap at everything?'

Ha ha ha.

The women climbed to their feet and Sofia crossed to the bin to clear up her mess. Marta wasn't sorry to see them go.

'Bye, Marta. See you.'

Marta waved.

'Bye, girls, it's been a pleasure.'

As the women disappeared into the vine-covered pergola Marta dug out her tablet, took the lid off her lunchbox and settled down to enjoy her salad in peace.

THREE

S itting on the tram, gazing up at the remnants of the old city walls, Marta felt at peace with herself and the world. Paolo's party sorted. A trip out to Petreni. Glorious weather. If only every day could be like this.

Pulling her Report Master from her satchel, she logged in to the VisionPlace intranet and took another look at the request.

'Roman House: Grade four...'

One below the best, she thought. Premium rental.

'...built between 1924–25 as an apartment block. Occupied during WWII by various army units. From 1943 onwards used as an officers' mess for Frontier Guard Division. July 1944 suffered minor bomb damage to the upper floors when American bombers overshot marshalling yards...'

Marta skipped the archive link for this incident and read on.

'...1947 – building transferred to municipal ownership and

used to house party officials and their families. After the '89 revolution property reverted to the city council. Acquired by VisionPlace 2023, since when the building has...'

Marta scrolled down to the current tenants.

'...Michael and Sophie Brancusi. Dependants 1. Steffi Brancusi, age 15.'

'Petreni one minute,' the locator announced. 'Enesco Petreni.'

Marta logged off and slipped the Report Master back inside her satchel before joining the short queue waiting at the rear exit. As the tram slowed she held on to the grab handle and looked out at the park running alongside, the white almond-blossoms lining its pathways, the hanging baskets heavy with geraniums and fuchsias. What must it be like to live in a place where saplings are left in the ground, she wondered, where flower baskets rather than CCTV cameras hang from the streetlamps?

Making her way down Nastase, Marta studied the beautiful window displays and marvelled at the extortionate prices in the chic boutiques. Five minutes later she arrived at the junction with Zal and paused to survey the building on the opposite corner. It was an impressive place, Roman House, four storeys tall and brick built with stone arches over the windows and ornate balconies on the upper floor. The lobby, some ten or fifteen metres past the traffic lights, was fronted entirely with tinted glass, enhancing the place's aura of exclusivity. Excited at the prospect of seeing inside she joined the group of people waiting for the lights to change.

Once through the security vestibule she was not disappointed. Having logged her ID with the receptionist, Marta was told that the concierge was on his way down and directed to a plush seating area. Whilst waiting she made a more thorough appraisal of the lobby, from the potted palms standing by the entrance to the intricate floral patterns on the wallpaper and the glossy holiday magazines fanned out across the table. She had not seen anything like this since Arpad took her to the Prince Nikolai in St Petersburg. It was another world, far, far away from the estates where her assessment work usually took her. No wonder the boys in Residential kept these visits for themselves, she thought, leafing through the photographs of timeshare apartments in Bali, Peru and—

'Miss Ionescu?'

Marta jumped and the magazine slipped from her grasp. The man standing before her, much older than his receptionist colleague and with gold braiding on the lapels of *his* plum jacket, bent down and picked up the magazine. The skin on the back of his bald, tanned head was wrinkled, like a dog's jowls.

'I'm sorry if I startled you, Miss,' he said, placing the magazine back on the table. 'Gyula Bokros, concierge.'

Marta stood up and offered her hand, which the man took in his white glove and shook limply.

'It's Ms actually...'

'Oh, I'm so sorry, *Ms* Ionescu,' the concierge said, wringing his hands. 'If you could just bear with me, I'll go and check that it's alright for us to go up.'

Marta got the distinct feeling that the concierge disapproved of her. Maybe he thought building maintenance was best left to the boys, or perhaps he would have been more comfortable if she had turned up in workwear and steel-capped boots. He wouldn't be the first and, no doubt, not the last. Either way it didn't bother her; she just got on with the job. She watched as he handed the phone back to the receptionist and started back towards her.

'Yes, it's OK, we can go up.'

They walked across to the lift and the concierge slid open two gates, concertina affairs like the ones in the old gangster movies Arpad collected. He motioned to her to step into the lift, then followed her in and closed the gates behind him. Marta was enchanted. With its wood half-panelling and single light bulb, the cabin was like a little time capsule. Their ascent was slow but remarkably smooth, leaving Marta time to inspect the thick carpets and gold-framed pictures beyond the metal caging. When the lift stopped the concierge pulled open the gates and stood aside for Marta to exit. She stepped out and inhaled the musky fragrance coming from the vase of pink roses standing on the table next to the staircase. No stench of piss-stained stairwells or old cooking oil here, thank you very much!

'This way,' Bokros said, waving at the door opposite.

He rang the bell and they waited in silence. When at last the door was opened Marta found herself staring up at a very tall, skinny man with a kindly face. Early forties, she reckoned.

'Good afternoon, sir. This is—'

'Marta Ionescu, Mr Brancusi,' she said, holding out her hand. 'Pleased to meet you.'

A firm, dry grip.

'Do come in,' Michael said, stepping aside.

'Thanks,' Marta replied, marvelling at the size of the place. The whole of her apartment would fit into the hallway she was now standing in. The décor was not for her though, all those gold-framed paintings and brass fittings, far too fussy.

'I need to make a couple of calls, sir,' the concierge said, trying to hide his annoyance at Marta's pushiness. 'Would you excuse me for a moment, please?'

'Sure, Gyula, go ahead,' Michael said. 'I can show Ms Ionescu what the problem is.'

He closed the apartment door to find Marta crouching beneath the skylight, inspecting the ruby carpet.

'We used a bucket,' Michael said, pointing at the stained area. 'Got the worst of it up with towels.'

'You've not had any trouble before?'

'No, nothing at all. Do you need any steps?'

17

'No, thanks. I just need to locate where the rain's getting in then I'll go and have a look up top.'

'Right, I'll leave you to it then. Give me a shout if you need anything.'

Michael continued on his way, disappearing behind the door at the far end of the hall. Marta heard a brief flurry of voices – the tenant and two women – then everything fell quiet again. Disturbingly so. Marta was so used to noise, to kids crying and couples arguing and dogs barking: the silence here was overpowering. But it wasn't the only thing that caught her attention; the stain on the carpet, with a series of silvery-blue rings fanning outwards like ripples in a pond, was also unusual. It looked more chemical than water, like oil or putty, but she knew from perusing the log on the way over that Maintenance hadn't been called out to this address for some time. Putting down her bag, she took out her Report Master and found, as suspected, that there was nothing recent in the log. The last job at Roman House – a lift repair – had been carried out the previous summer. The Brancusis' apartment had had nothing done since November 2028, nearly eighteen months ago.

Intrigued, Marta took out her palmcom and inspected the skylight directly above the stain. Zooming in, she quickly found what she was looking for: a snail's trail running from the bottom of the frame and down the plastered ceiling well, some forty-odd centimetres. After photographing this she scanned left and right for further evidence of any leaks. Finding nothing she moved to the opposite side of the hall and repeated the process. That done, she picked up the Report Master once more and started dictating her findings. When she had finished she packed away her things and was about to go and tap on the door when Michael reappeared.

'Everything OK?'

'Yes, fine, thanks, Mr Brancusi. I'm going up onto the roof now and shouldn't need to trouble you again. Someone will be along in the next hour or two with a tarpaulin and you'll be notified first thing tomorrow about the actual repairs. In the meantime, here's my card. Please feel free to call me if you have any further problems.'

Michael pocketed the card and walked Marta down to the door.

'Goodbye,' he said as they shook hands. 'And thank you.'

Marta smiled and stepped out into the corridor. The door closed.

She found Bokros pacing around and talking into his palmcom further along the corridor. The concierge ended his call and scowled at Marta.

'All done?'

'Yeah. I'd like to see up top now, please.'

'Of course. This way.'

He led her through a doorway marked 'Fire Escape' and on to a concrete staircase in an unplastered shaft where the coarse, dusty brickwork contrasted sharply with the building's luxurious interior. After climbing two short flights of steps they stopped before the exit door and concierge Bokros tapped a code into the grimy keypad beside it before pushing on the bar and stepping out onto the roof. Marta reached for her sunglasses; the light outside was ferocious. The view, though, was fantastic: old tiled roofs and patterned chimneys, stylish office and apartment blocks soaring high above the narrow streets.

The skylight was some twenty metres away. Having negotiated a path through the forest of aerials, ventilation pipes and satellite dishes, Marta crouched down to inspect the seals, relieved when the grumpy concierge lit a cigarette and wandered off to talk on his palmcom. She soon discovered what the problem was: some filler around a glass unit on the upright section of the skylight had recently been renewed and there was a tiny slit along the bottom edge where the still spongy material had receded. To confirm her diagnosis she went round to the opposite side of the skylight and scanned the plaster in the ceiling well with her palmcom. Sure enough, there beneath the repaired section was the snail trail she had spotted earlier. After taking a few photographs she reached for her Report Master and logged back in, intrigued. There was unlikely to be an error with the log itself: the maintenance team's bonus depended on the number of jobs successfully completed so it was in their interest to ensure that everything was correctly recorded. So why was there no entry? It was a lousy repair job, too, hastily completed. The machine pinged, it was ready to receive her report.

'Enter Inspection Log,' Marta began. 'Roman House, Petreni, Apartment 301. Thursday March twenty-first, twenty-thirty. Leaking skylight, inspection by—'

'Found anything?' Bokros asked, having silently reappeared at her side.

'Yes. I'll show you.'

Marta put down the Report Master and led Bokros around to the other side of the skylight, where she knelt down beside the faulty unit.

'The filler here's been renewed but there's a small fissure in it, see? This is where the water's getting in.'

The concierge frowned.

'That's strange, I don't recall any repairs.'

'Hmm… Tell me, is all the maintenance work here done by VisionPlace?'

Judging by the look on the concierge's face, she might just as well have asked him if he was a child molester.

'Of course. Do you think the tenants here pay a premium rent to have some cash-cowboy look after things?'

'No, I'm sure they don't, it's just that… well, there's no record of this skylight being repaired, and that filler is pretty new. Less than a month, I'd say. Look.'

Marta prodded the spongy filler with the end of her pen.

'See what I mean?'

They stared at each other, working through the implications of her discovery.

'There is another possibility. Have the Brancusis reported a break-in recently?'

The concierge shook his head.

'No,' he said. 'No way.'

Marta could see that he wasn't enjoying her questions, but she needed to sort this out, and quickly. Maintenance would be waiting for her to file her report. She looked back at the intruder detector in the corner of the ceiling well.

'Is the alarm down there linked to the apartment's security circuit or the building's?'

'The apartment's.'

That's weird, she told herself. The family would surely know whether or not they had had intruders. Unless of course they hadn't noticed anything missing.

'I need to speak with Mr Brancusi again. I think the place might have been burgled.'

'Burgled? You think a bunch of dwarves slipped in through there?'

Marta pulled out her tape measure and crouched down again to measure the glass unit.

'Forty-five centimetres: I could get through there, easy.'

'Even if you could, the moment the unit was removed the alarm would go off.'

'There are ways of neutralising detectors, you know that.'

The concierge inflated his chest.

'Look, *Ms* Ionescu. No-one farts in this building without me knowing. If—'

'Listen. VisionPlace is accountable to its clients and I'm accountable to VisionPlace. And what if the family haven't noticed anything missing because they haven't looked?'

Bokros maintained his rigid, defensive posture, but his face softened.

'OK. Look, I'll speak to Mr Brancusi.'

'Thank you. I'll pack up here and head back. If you could let me know—'

'Sure. As soon as I've spoken to him.'

The concierge turned and headed back towards the fire escape door. Marta lingered, thinking about what he had said, about what to do for the best. As a police helicopter flew overhead, the heavy thrum of its blades bouncing off the surrounding chimney stacks, she looked down once more. Only this time her focus moved beyond the glass to an object some three or four metres below, a face staring up at her. It was a beautiful young woman, a teenager, her golden hair hanging across her shoulders. Seen through the dusty glass she reminded Marta of a woman in the picturebook bible she had as a kid, that golden halo, those sad, imploring eyes. Then she was gone and Marta, in youth worker mode, wondered what it was that was so vexing the poor girl. Boyfriend trouble? Cyber-bullying? Parental conflict?

'Ms Ionescu,' Bokros called. 'Are you coming?'

*

Marta heard voices inside the apartment, the sound of bolts being slid. Slowly the door opened and clunked against the security wedge and Aunt Lisha's wizened face appeared around the side.

'Hello, dear,' she said, peering over her spectacles at her niece before stamping on the wedge and opening the door wide.

'Hello, Auntie,' Marta replied, stepping into the apartment and kissing her aunt's downy cheek.

Aunt Lisha closed the door.

'Coffee? Chocolate?'

'No thanks, Auntie, I can't stay long.'

She hung her jacket on the rail and turned around to discover her mother waiting for her at the far end of the hall, bent and frowning.

'Always in a hurry, girl. You want to slow down, you'll give yourself a heart attack.'

Marta picked up her satchel and sauntered down the hallway, determined not to take the bait.

'Heart and lung function of a teenager, Mama, or so my last company check-up reckoned.'

She kissed her mother on the cheek. 'Whatever I die of I doubt it'll be a heart attack.'

Through in the pensioners' cramped living room traditional folk dances were playing on the radio and the net curtains swayed in the mild evening breeze, carrying in the pungent scent of acetone from the nearby paint factory. Marta retrieved a half-dozen dog-eared and musty paperbacks from her bag and placed them on the table. Her mother shuffled in behind her, sat down and took a book from the top of the pile. Seeing the old woman lick her fingers as she started leafing through the soiled pages made Marta feel nauseous. She passed a book to her aunt, now sitting on the worn settee, and dropped down beside her.

'"Doomed to a life of serfdom,"' Aunt Lisha began, reading the cover. '"Anna believed she would never be rescued. Until one day a new Chief of Security arrived at the palace." *How* exciting,' she said, not bothering to conceal the sarcasm in her voice.

'At least I can still read whole sentences,' Marta's mother sneered.

'Sure, as long as the words aren't more than two syllables long.'

'Pah!'

FOUR

Gyula Bokros kept his word, g-mailing Marta first thing the following day to confirm that the tenant and his family had no reason to suspect they had been burgled. Nothing was missing, everything seemed in order: *The detector in the ceiling well has been tested and is working. Maybe someone tried to break in and then thought better of it. Either way, without any evidence to the contrary, let's draw a line under this matter, shall we? Oh, and by the way, your Maintenance people arrived just eighty-seven minutes after you left and re-sealed the whole unit. The tenants are delighted. Thank you for your speedy and most effective intervention.*

Another satisfied customer!

Marta was on an early shift that Friday and, apart from fielding the occasional customer query or complaint, continued with the loathed month-end return. Sadly, Dina was on a day off; time always went more slowly when her friend wasn't around. In the end, Marta managed to get away soon after four-thirty, intending to meet a handful of her volunteer colleagues at St Vincent's in order to put up the decorations and prepare the buffet for Paolo's party. When, sitting on the tram into town, her palmcom started buzzing she had no idea that her plans for Friday were about to change big time. Slipping her hand inside her pocket she pulled out the phone and almost jumped off the seat. It was a message from Arpad.

'Hi, hon, I'm back. Fancy a bite at Revolution tonight?'

Her boyfriend's early return from Brussels was the best surprise she could have wished for. Their last meeting had not gone well and she wanted to do something to halt the sense of drift creeping into their relationship, to recapture the fun and romance that had filled their first year together. She dictated a prompt reply, hoping it would send the right signal:

'You bet! I'm at the club tonight but could get to R for ten-thirty. OK?'

Maybe things would be better now they had spent a few days apart. *Oh Christ, I hope so. Please let it be right.*

*

St Vincent's community hall had seen better days but that evening Marta and her fellow volunteers gave the dowdy space an impressive makeover. While one team hung coloured balloons and bunting from the rafters and draped a huge maroon and canary banner (Paolo's college team colours) across the back wall – 'WELL DONE, PAOLO – GOVAL'S HERO' – another laid out jugs of fruit juice and an abundance of home-made nibbles on two pasting tables covered with the remnants of the banner fabric. Later on, all hands to the pump, they shifted the table tennis and pool tables to one side to clear a space in the centre of the room for dancing.

When Enver, the giant Brightbeam Security guard, opened the doors at seven-thirty and the kids wandered in to discover the decorations and buffet, Marta was thrilled to see the look on the youngsters' faces. The way they made a beeline for the food you'd have thought none of them had eaten in days. Or maybe, Marta hoped, it was just that the food was free. Whatever, the atmosphere was unusually calm from the off, which was exactly what she had hoped for. Earlier that afternoon she had called Angela, Paolo's mother, and asked her to stall the family's arrival until after eight so that she could get everyone fed and watered and deal with any pressing personal issues. Sure enough, by the time Paolo and his parents arrived, the place was buzzing: a gang of teenage girls and some of the younger boys were dancing to the music blasting out from the club's ancient Hi-Fi; Enver and a group of raucous lads were playing pool; and, in the far corner, two headscarf-wearing sisters were noisily battling their volunteer opponents on the games screens. Ion rushed straight over to join the dancers, his exaggerated attempts to ape their movements prompting howls of laughter. But Paolo proved far and away the main attraction and before long a small crowd had gathered around the sofas at the back of the hall to hear the footballing hero's account of his team's recent victory.

'I knew we could do it,' he told his audience, grinning and waving his arms. 'Once we put the second one away they just gave up.'

The lad's popularity was evident in the admiring looks on his listeners' faces. Even Father Jozsef, who had dropped by to carry out his bi-weekly club check-up, briefly joined the congregation, until the buffet – or what was left of it – tempted him away. As always when the priest arrived, Marta made herself scarce. Despite her not having been to Mass or confession for more than five years, Father Jozsef had never given up trying to coax her back or, worse, convince her mother that Marta's soul was in peril. Later, after the priest had left, Marta made a short speech and presented Paolo with a sportswear voucher. Everyone clapped and cheered and popped streamers. Years later, Marta would look back at this evening as one of the happiest moments in her life.

At nine forty-five, Marta stood outside the hall saying goodnight to the kids as they headed off into the dark. Paolo emerged, elated, his proud parents in tow, and gave Marta a hug.

'Thanks, Marta, it's been brilliant.'

'No more than you deserve.'

Angela and Marta exchanged kisses.

'I tell him how lucky he is to have this place, Marta. And you.'

'It's true, Marta,' Ion added. 'You work miracles with these kids.'

'Get off with you. Any more of that and I won't be able to get back through the door.'

The Gheorghius laughed and sauntered off down the path, the three of them arm in arm.

Marta turned to Enver.

'Right, I'm going to get changed.'

'Take your time, Marta, I ain't in no hurry,' Enver said, pulling a cigarette packet from his uniform pocket as Marta disappeared inside. After lighting his cigarette the big man wandered down the path to the gate and looked up and down the road. Fewer than half the streetlights were working and most of the inhabitants in the surrounding apartment blocks had closed their blinds for the night. Enver listened to the high-pitched whine of a speeding motorbike, kids shouting and whistling in the distance, before turning away and drifting back up the path.

*

When Marta emerged from the church hall, Enver was dumbfounded. Tonight, as usual, she had worn jeans and a T-shirt to the club. Now here she was dressed in a backless black and silver striped dress, a peacock feather shawl over her shoulders, diamante clutch bag in her hand.

'Wow, Marta,' he said, stepping on his cigarette, 'you look great. Lucky guy.'

'Thanks, Enver,' she replied with an awkward smile, opening her purse and taking out a note. 'Listen, would you mind giving the girls a hand clearing up when I've gone? Flori's got the key.'

Enver waved the note away.

'Happy to help,' he said. 'You don't need to pay me.'

They turned and headed down the path.

'Well, that all seemed to go off OK,' she said. 'And Paolo looked so happy.'

'Yeah, I like it when the kids are good. Ain't no need to behave like animals all the time.'

Marta laughed.

'I wish it was that straightforward!'

As they stepped out onto the pavement Marta's palmcom buzzed. She took the device from her bag and tapped the screen. It was the taxi.

'He's just turned off Meresti. Two minutes.'

Enver smiled and nodded his head. He said something but his words were obscured by a passing ambulance's siren. Marta liked having him around. Of all the guards Brightbeam supplied he was by far the most patient. The cops who patrolled the estate hassled and bullied the kids but Enver actually seemed to enjoy working with them. They respected him, too: no-one, not even the toughest, messed with him. As if that was not bonus enough, he always insisted on walking her home or, if she was going out, keeping her company while she waited for her taxi. Not something covered by the contract, of course, but she wasn't going to complain. He never came on to her or asked for anything in return, he was just one of those rare people who seemed to enjoy doing favours. Given the state of Goval's streets these days, she was deeply grateful for that.

'It's really good of you to keep me company, Enver, I do appreciate it.'

The big man grinned.

'No problem, Marta, I ain't got no date tonight.'

A battered petrol Volkswagen with a taxi sign on the roof turned into the street and drew up in front of them. Marta was pleased to see Tony de Columbus sitting at the wheel. Given the rapid turnover of drivers in this part of town and their increasingly lousy grasp of the city's geography, she much preferred being driven by Comfy Cars' owner. Besides, he was a really funny guy, forever trying to shock her with some piece of gossip. Years back, not long after she had arrived in Goval, he had asked her out. He'd changed the subject pretty sharpish, though, when she had asked innocently whether or not his wife and kids would be joining them. There were few secrets in Goval in those days. Things were different now.

Enver opened the taxi's rear door.

'Thank you, kind sir,' she said, lowering her head and climbing inside. 'May see you next week then?'

'I sure hope so. You enjoy yourself now.'

He closed the door with a firm clunk and Marta sat back in her seat and pulled on her seatbelt.

'Hi, Tony.'

As the taxi moved off, the driver's voice materialised over the speaker set in the corner of the screen.

'Hi, Marta. Adrian's, is it?'

'No way, no slumming for me tonight... Revolution.'

'Heh, fan-cy. Your birthday or somethin'?'

'No, just a quiet, romantic meal.'

Tony whistled.

'Cosy.'

They waited at the Meresti Street junction for a gap in the traffic.

'So how was the kids tonight?'

'They were really good. We had a bit of a celebration for Paolo.'

Tony's eyes met Marta's in the rear-view mirror.

'Paolo Gheorghiu?'

'Yep.'

'Wow. Great feet, that kid, Dynamo should snap him up. Good role model, too. Too much aggro, most kids these days.'

'Oh, they're not all bad… Anyhow, why don't we ever see your two at St Vincent's anymore?'

'Listen, I ain't got no idea what goes on in those girls' heads. They don't speak to me one day to the next. I try to talk to them, they look at me like dirt.'

Marta laughed; she had heard Tony's grumpy parent routine many times over the years.

Out on the city highway, her excitement growing, Marta gazed at the passing warehouses and factories, the floodlit freight yard and Jump City with its pallet-shacks and tarpaulin wigwams, home to an army of transients. Down the hill they drove, beneath Dynamo's glittering new stadium and into the city proper, along Enesco with its silver apartment blocks and classy window displays, all those taillights up ahead blinking like swarms of fireflies. She loved the city at night. Where she had grown up there were no streetlights or holo-ads, just a few humble cottages in the middle of fields that stretched to the horizon, two dozen families living cheek by jowl sharing harvests and holidays, snow and dust, a universe away from this anonymous world of nigh on a half million people bound together by concrete and steel and money. Tonight she was going to pull out all the stops. If things did not work out it would not be for want of trying.

Marta found herself back at her friend Elena's wedding and her first meeting with the bride's cousin, Arpad, a gorgeous hunk wearing a mohair suit and Italian shoes. A fortnight later, on their first date, he had taken her to Revolution, the best restaurant in Caradea. She had never experienced food like it. That night, at his apartment, they had become lovers and her tranquil existence had been transformed. Theirs had never been a conventional association like the ones the women at work were always going on about: romance, engagement, marriage, kids. Arpad was a busy man with a life of his own, a life seemingly dominated by an unending series of palmcom conversations and mysterious meetings at the oddest of hours. The construction business, he told her, was all about making deals: wooing the client, undercutting the competition, landing the contract. And that took information, information that came from all sorts of contacts, day and night. Marta was fascinated; she longed to hear more, but Arpad rarely discussed his business with her.

'Let's not waste our time talking about work,' he would always say whenever she showed an interest. 'There's so much more in life to enjoy.'

And so she grew to accept their unorthodox arrangement, the late-night trysts at his spotless loft in Ticha with its plump sofas and Turkish rugs, lolling about in their dressing gowns watching movies on his huge comscreen. German chocolates and French champagne, the most attentive love-making she'd ever known. To the woman who had never entirely shed her country roots he remained an enigma. But that only made him more desirable.

Marta couldn't recall a specific incident or moment when her relationship with Arpad had changed. It had simply dawned on her one night, early in the new year when she and Dina had gone out for a drink and got to talking about men, that they had been drifting for some time. There had been no big drama or falling-out, just the occasional stifled yawn, the odd little quip. They were both drinking heavily and the sex had become more mechanical, less spontaneous. Perhaps he was tiring of her, maybe she no longer pleased him as she once did, who knows? On the one occasion when she had tried to broach the subject with him he'd just shrugged his shoulders and grumbled about work, claimed he was worried sick about the latest round of federal budget cuts. Marta, meanwhile, could summon neither the energy to change things nor the courage to do without what little affection he still offered.

The taxi slowed as they neared the restaurant and Marta shivered, sensing a dramatic shift in the air around her, like the approaching thunderstorms of her childhood. Moments later they pulled up in front of Revolution and a burly, black-suited attendant wearing an earpiece sprang forward to get the door.

'Thanks, Tony,' she said, laying a twenty in the pay drawer and pulling her shawl around her shoulders. 'See you.'

Tony retrieved the note and waved. He was discreet enough not to ask whether she needed picking up.

'Enjoy your meal, Marta.'

She stepped out onto the pavement and crossed to the glass doors which swung open on her approach. Inside the lobby, with its sumptuous carpet and glittering chandelier, the immaculately groomed major-domo stepped forward from behind his lectern and bowed. She remembered this gorgeous Frenchman from her first visit.

'Good evening, Mademoiselle. You have a reservation?'

'I'm meeting Mr Radics.'

'Of course. This way, please.'

Marta followed the man into the dining area, a long room packed with smartly dressed diners sitting beneath a canopy of red, yellow and blue silk, the colours of the old national flag. She had forgotten all about the garish mural running around the walls that had prompted Arpad's lecture on the revolution.

'It's not just about a dictator's overthrow,' he had told her, waving at the walls, 'it's a celebration of the people's revolt against forty years of endless shortages and state-sponsored violence.'

That sudden flash of steely-eyed, chin-jutting pride had impressed her. Of course, at thirty five, just two years older than her, he wasn't even born when the Great Father and Mother were dragged from their marble palace, a trick of time that even the worldly Arpad could not reverse…

She could see him now, over by the far wall, grinning and waving and looking very dapper in his silver-grey suit.

'Your waiter this evening will be Teodor, Mademoiselle,' the major-domo said when they arrived at the table. A florid-faced little man with a broad smile approached and pulled out the chair for Marta.

'Hello, darling,' Arpad said, getting to his feet and kissing her on the lips. Marta laid her bag on the table next to the vase of short-stemmed chrysanthemums and sat down. The waiter asked what she would like to drink.

'Champagne,' Arpad said, taking Marta's hand. 'We're celebrating.'

The waiter inclined his head and disappeared. Arpad leaned towards her, his hennaed fringe flopping down over his forehead.

'You look great, Marta,' he said. 'I've really missed you.'

Marta was delighted; things had got off to a good start.

'So, how was Brussels?'

'Great! We got the job.'

'Oh, that's brilliant, Arpad! Are you going to tell me what is it now?'

He grinned, acknowledging her rebuke.

'Building more Welcome Homes – Budapest, Novi Sad, Craiova. Maybe others.'

'I thought Regional Governments' budgets were being cut?'

'They are, but this programme's fire-proof. Brussels is desperate to bring the Union's workforce mobility up to American and Chinese levels. Hostels like these, especially so many, will help.'

Workforce mobility? To Marta it meant just one thing: the further weakening of communities already under pressure. She saw the results every week in the club: fathers or siblings away from home for months at a time, kids often not in one place long enough to complete a school year. But she and Arpad had argued over such things before and doubtless would do again. Tonight was not the time to rekindle such debates.

'That's great news.'

The waiter arrived with the champagne, eased out the cork and filled their glasses with an accuracy and briskness that belied the man's somewhat frayed appearance.

'Congratulations,' she said, raising her glass. 'Here's to your continued success.'

'To *our* continued success,' he replied with a wink.

FIVE

Marta eased open her eyes and squinted at her dress and stockings, draped over the chair in the corner, bathed in the half-light seeping out from behind the bedroom curtains. Her head throbbed and her lips were glued together: God, what a night! Reaching for her palmcom she read 07.49; thank God she was on a day off! Hearing Arpad's gentle snoring she turned carefully and peered across at the outline of him beneath the duvet, lying on his side, his back turned towards her. He'd been on dazzling form last night, grinning from ear to ear as he recounted how he'd wined and dined a succession of MEPs, the glitzy ceremony at which his company's success had been announced. The most thrilling event of the trip had nothing to do with the Welcome Homes contract, though, he insisted, but the discovery of one of the earliest gangster movies ever made – the uncut version of a silent movie called *Underworld* – on his hotel's in-house entertainment system. Marta knew precious little about Arpad's work but she had heard plenty about what he called his 'interests': assembling a library of classic gangster movies and buying and selling fine samurai figurines.

'You mean there's a gangster movie you *haven't* got?' she'd joshed, amused by the lengths to which Arpad would go to satisfy his weird obsessions.

'Sure, there are three,' he'd said, laughing. 'Well, two now. I slipped the night porter a fifty to mail me a copy.'

He'd even suggested, during the short taxi ride from the restaurant to his place, that they watch the damned film. Marta was having none of that, though. How easy it had been to divert him… Another snort from Arpad, a bout of shuffling and groaning, interrupted Marta's reverie, prompting her to slip from the bed, pull on his dressing gown and tiptoe from the room.

After making herself a coffee Marta went through to the loft apartment's huge lounge area and spread herself across one of the sofas. With its Turkish rugs, modern-art posters and Arpad's treasured collection of bronze and terracotta warriors occupying the glass-fronted cabinets lining the long wall opposite the windows, this was one of her favourite places, somewhere she always felt pampered and safe. As she savoured the delicious coffee and absorbed the room's serenity she could feel her headache retreating. Picking up the remote she activated the huge comscreen at the far end of the room and found herself staring at the mobster and his moll from the black and white film Arpad had started watching last night. Swiftly exiting the movie archive she scrolled through Arpad's files, searching for the photos of Elena's wedding in the grounds of the swanky Prince Constantin hotel. She soon found what she was looking for and scrolled happily through the images: the two of them deep in conversation, joking with the bride and groom, dancing together beneath the lanterns. Everyone is smiling, what a special day…

Marta paused and her face clouded over. Swinging her legs from the sofa she sat up and studied the screen, confused as to the connection between the wedding and the photos now appearing, a series of what look like surveillance shots of a young woman, seemingly unaware she is being photographed, hurrying along a street, buying a coffee, sitting in a car with another older woman, blonde and expensively dressed. Marta recognised the subject in the photographs but couldn't place her… Then she realised it was the missing Ukranian woman, Ludmilla Fedoruk. But what was—

'She's a good-looking woman, eh…'

Marta, startled, span around to see Arpad standing in the doorway in his vest and boxer shorts.

'…I hope they find her.'

'Arpad, hi. I… I was just looking at the photos of Elena's wedding.'

Arpad crossed the carpet and dropped down on the sofa beside Marta. He eased the remote from her hand and placed it on the coffee table.

'ARCHIVE. BACKSPACE ELEVEN.'

The comscreen flashed up another photo, the newly married Elena and her husband posing for photos outside the wedding chapel. Marta felt uneasy, unsure what she had stumbled upon, at a loss as to what to say. Arpad turned to her, a big smile on his face.

'What a great day,' he said, giving her hand a squeeze.

Marta pulled her hand away and nodded at the screen.

'So what's with…?'

'I'm sorry, Marta, you shouldn't have seen those.'

He paused, his eyes settling on hers.

'Listen, I'm going to tell you something but you must swear never to repeat a word. Promise?'

Marta hesitated. Where was all this heading?

'Promise me,' Arpad insisted.

'Sure. Whatever, just tell me.'

Arpad scanned her face, appearing to wrestle with some inner voice.

'I work for the government,' he began at last. 'In border security.'

Marta, astonished, waited for Arpad to continue. *This is insane.*

'For some time now we've been tracking a gang of people

traffickers operating out of Ukraine. We believe this woman is involved.'

'But, on the news they reckoned she'd been trafficked herself.'

Arpad snorted.

'Don't believe everything you hear on the news, Marta. That's just cover.'

'So… Where is she now?'

'We don't know. When she realised we were on to her she left her job and her apartment and just disappeared. But we'll find her, sooner or—'

'So that's why all the weird hours, the late-night calls. The travel.'

Arpad nodded thoughtfully.

'Some of it, yeah, but not all. The construction business, the Welcome Homes, Brussels, all of that's true. That's what I did before I was recruited and still do.'

'Your cover?'

'Exactly.'

Marta picked up her mug and finished the remnants of her lukewarm coffee. She was quaking inside; her whole world had been turned upside down.

'Go on,' she said, struggling to control her voice.

SIX

A top-of-the-range electric taxi pulled up outside the converted warehouse, headlamps on, wipers sweeping streams of water from the windscreen. Marta and Arpad dashed from the building's entrance and across the pavement, Arpad holding aloft an umbrella that offered scant protection, Marta clutching her shawl to her throat, her dress tight to her thighs. Arpad opened the vehicle's rear door and Marta clambered aboard, turning to exchange a chaste kiss with her lover before sliding onto the seat and pulling on her seatbelt. Arpad closed the door and tapped on the front passenger window. After exchanging a few words with the driver he reached in and swiped his palmcom over the auto-toll before giving Marta a quick wave and dashing back inside.

In the silent rear compartment, Marta gazed absent-mindedly out the window as the taxi floated through Ticha's old commercial quarter. Arpad had always been a bit of a mystery to her but... Undercover cop? Secret agent? He'd never previously struck her as a fantasist and God knows she'd met a few of those over the years. But the more she chewed over what he had told her, the more uneasy she felt. Even if he was telling the truth, the thought that their current lifestyle would not be changing anytime soon demolished her dreams of marriage and kids… Uncertain and anxious, Marta focussed afresh on the city centre's passing sights, the rain-swept Hapsburg façades, the Baroque statues and fountains…

'Why are we going this way?'

The driver stared hard at Marta in the rear-view mirror.

'They've closed Agricola Square. How else am I gonna get to Goval?'

Marta registered the taxis and buses slowing up ahead.

'Has there been an accident?'

'You haven't heard the news?'

'What news?'

The taxi came to a halt behind stationary traffic.

'About the bomb? At Union House?'

Marta lurched forward.

'Union House?'

'Yeah, last night.'

For the second time that morning Marta couldn't believe what she was hearing.

'Jesus.'

'Lucky there was only two people in the place.'

Marta fumbled with her clutch bag, took out her palmcom and started tapping furiously, swiping through the pictures of Union House: the building's white plaster streaked with smoke stains, its windows blown out; firemen spraying water onto the still smouldering upper storeys; piles of charred and buckled furniture lying in the street. Shocked, she tapped her palmcom again and discovered a long list of missed calls, including several from her mother and Dina, and two from David. She tapped David's latest call and her fraught-looking boss promptly appeared.

'God, am I glad to see you. I thought you might be away for the weekend.'

'I can't believe it, after all the work we put in on the refurb.'

'I know. Look, things are going crazy here so I'll cut to the chase. Can you come in?'

'You mean, like today?'

'I mean, like now.'

Marta was rattled. Her headache had returned with a vengeance; her mouth was dry.

'Yeah, sure. I need to get home first though, feed Gypsy, get changed.'

She checked her wristwatch.

'I can be with you by... eleven?'

'OK, thanks, Marta. If you can make it sooner that'd be great.'

The screen went blank. Marta sat back in her seat, dazed, and stared out at the snarled-up traffic. The driver had switched on his radio and she could hear the news coming over the speaker link, a woman reporting from the scene.

'...The emergency services have confirmed that at least one person, believed to be a UES employee, died in the blast. Meanwhile, the Regional Commissioner is due to visit the site this afternoon...'

*

In the end it was gone midday by the time Marta joined David in his office. Out of breath and fuming, she hung her satchel and umbrella on the coatstand and dropped onto one of the chairs at the meeting table where her boss was sitting, poring over reams of print-outs.

'I'm sorry, David, town's at a standstill and the taxi—'

'Forget it,' David snapped, clearly flustered. 'Sorry, it's been a bit of a madhouse here... So, Frankfurt's got a team of engineers on stand-by. The minute they get the all-clear they'll be flying in to assess the damage and the building's viability. The Board's keen to start reconstruction, or rebuilding, ASAP.'

'I still don't understand, why would anyone want to bomb Union House?'

David shrugged his shoulders exaggeratedly.

'God knows, there're so many fucking crazies out there.'

'Have they released the name of the person who was killed yet?'

'No, there's been no word on that and, right now, I'm afraid our focus has to be elsewhere. We've been given the job of finding accommodation for all the client's employees.'

Marta was perplexed.

'But surely that's the lessee's responsibility?'

David sighed. He'd clearly been around this loop already.

'Normally that's the case, sure. But there's a special clause in the UES contract, to do with maintaining essential government services. Basically, we're obliged to do all we can to help them find suitable alternatives. Pronto. And, as I'm sure you're aware, pretty much our entire commercial stock is either occupied or under development.'

Marta snickered.

'So what are we supposed to do, approach our competitors?'

'Yes, that's exactly what *you'll* be doing.'

'Me?'

'You know the place better than any other support officer in this building and you did some great work on the refurbishment. What's more, I can trust you to do a good job.'

David's praise, extravagant by his standards, sent a wave of pride rolling through Marta's body. Suddenly, Arpad's confession and the logjammed city streets were forgotten.

'When do I start?' she asked, gripped by the prospect of a brand new challenge.

'Straightaway.'

'But what about the monthly return?'

'Forward everything to Andrea Rosu, I've already briefed her. I've also mailed you a few suggestions from the management team and booked the meeting room. For as long as you need it...'

For the first time that afternoon, David smiled.

'…Help minimise the distractions from Dina and co, eh! Any questions?'

'How long have I got?'

'Three days, four tops.'

Marta stood up.

'I'm on it.'

SEVEN

arta had put on a brave, 'you-can-rely-on-me' face for David but, once she was alone, cocooned in the meeting room, the reality of the situation hit home hard. All that work on the refurbishment, the hours she'd put in, the people she had met and with whom she'd built such fruitful relationships. She was sad, yes, but angry, too. She'd poured her heart and soul into that job and now it had all gone up in smoke at the whim of some religious or political lunatic...

One of the first calls Marta made that afternoon, once she had calmed down, was to Claudia Lacroix. Thankfully, Claudia and her team were safe, if somewhat shaken by events. As for the identity of the individual killed in the explosion, she claimed that the company was keeping that under wraps for now. After briefly considering the horrors that would doubtless have resulted had the bomb gone off in the daytime when the offices were open and fully staffed, the two women moved on to discuss what equipment and facilities would be needed for the interim accommodation. Marta pointed out that Brussels' push for a single building, rather than distributing the various teams around the region, was a big ask. She had a list of locations in front of her right now that, together, could accommodate some seventy per cent of the people displaced. The no-nonsense Claudia was quick to point out, however, what Marta already knew, that such a single location would benefit VisionPlace, too.

'After all, you will be responsible for the security and support at each location for months, maybe years to come,' the Frenchwoman said. 'Spreading the teams over a dozen or more locations would be infinitely more expensive and far less efficient in terms of the allocation of resources.'

After sending over some additional files from the refurbishment, and insisting that Marta contact her at any time should she need further assistance, Claudia signed off.

Relieved that her colleague and her team were unharmed, Marta pushed the bombing to the back of her mind. Little changed over the next day and a half as potential sites were identified and, once investigated more thoroughly, deemed to be inadequate. A distraction came unexpectedly on Monday afternoon, however, when a newsflash appeared on the meeting room comscreen: 'IDENTITY OF EMPLOYEE KILLED IN UNION HOUSE BOMB BLAST REVEALED.' Scanning the newsclip Marta immediately recognised the name of the deceased: Sophie Brancusi, a human rights lawyer in the Union's Regional secretariat. After revisiting her log and making further checks, Marta confirmed that this was indeed the wife of the tenant – Michael Brancusi – she had met at Roman House the previous week and, presumably, mother of the mournful-looking teenager she had spotted beneath the skylight. Gazing at the screen snatches she had taken of the newsflash, Marta felt overwhelmed by a profound sadness. *How does any partner – worse, any child – cope with being on the receiving end of such appalling news?*

*

Marta struck gold just after noon on the Wednesday, securing accommodation for the two hundred and thirty-two displaced

UES employees in a half-finished office block out at West Parks, the city's western transport interchange. The location in the bag, she spent the next few days working with VisionPlace's engineers on the plans for installing the necessary networks and workstations and, along with David, meeting a handful of private security companies to discuss arrangements for the protection of the site. The long spells spent working in isolation, the fourteen-hour shifts, the endless phone calls, cajoling and calling in of favours, had left her exhausted, desperate for the three days' leave her boss had offered her. But there was one more job to be done before she went home and fell into bed. Last year, given the state of her mother's health, Marta had promised herself that she would try and make the most of their time together, infuriating though the old lady could so often be. Since then, on the two or three Sundays each month when she was not working, Marta went for lunch with her mother and Aunt Lisha at their apartment just a ten-minute walk from her place. Unsure when the next such opportunity would arise, she called her mother and invited herself to supper.

*

Marta was relieved when Aunt Lisha opened the apartment door, allowing the sweet, peppery scent of her mother's chicken soup to spill out into the corridor and counteract the nauseating stench of cabbage and disinfectant that never left the run-down hallway.

'Goodness, you look terrible,' her aunt said as Marta stepped inside.

'Thanks a bunch, Auntie,' she laughed. 'I'm fine, just stupid busy, that's all.'

After hanging her bag and jacket on the rail Marta followed Aunt Lisha down the hall to the living room where her mother was sitting in her usual place at the table. The old woman frowned.

'Goodness, girl, you're pale as a goat. And your eyes… What happened, did someone punch you?'

'I've double-shifted for nine days straight, Mama,' she said, leaning down to deliver a kiss. 'I'm whacked.'

Marta flopped down on the settee and let out a long sigh.

'So you've found them all a place then,' Mrs Ionescu said, pulling out the battered tobacco pouch she kept in her apron pocket.

'Yep, at West Parks. It's being kitted out as we speak.'

'Well done, Marta,' Aunt Lisha said, heading through to the kitchen to fill the old tin kettle. 'Chocolate?'

'Please.'

'I hope they're paying you for all this extra work,' Mrs Ionescu said.

'Sure, Mama, overtime at weekends. I don't work for love!'

Her mother lay a cigarette paper on the table and started shredding tobacco over it. 'Talking of which, how's your fancy man? The one you're too ashamed to bring round.'

Marta hated it when her mother went on like this, punishing her for her failure to find herself a husband and provide her with the grandchildren she claimed to crave.

'You know how busy Arpad is, Mama. I'll bring him round again when things quieten down, I promise.'

'Leave her be, Ele,' Aunt Lisha tutted. 'You can see she's out on her feet.'

The three women fell silent. Mrs Ionescu smoked her cigarette, gazing into space and picking tobacco from between her stained teeth whilst her sister-in-law pottered in the kitchen. Marta picked up the church magazine and scanned the ads. She regretted not going home for a nap first but knew that she'd probably never have got up again if she'd gone anywhere near a bed. God, she felt so weary…

'Here you are, dear,' Aunt Lisha said, handing her niece a glass beaker in a plastic holder.

Marta tossed the magazine aside and savoured the delicious smell of her aunt's hot chocolate.

'Thanks, Auntie. Anyhow, how have *you* both been keeping?'

'Oh, the same as usual,' her mother replied. 'No better, no—'

'Hah,' Aunt Lisha interrupted. 'She's been sulking, ever since Father Jozsef complimented Mrs Antall on her dress.'

'Nonsense,' Mrs Ionescu said. 'If the man's too stupid to know when a woman is flirting with him, who am I to worry? Anyhow, forget him,' she ordered, her head wreathed in smoke.

Marta nodded, hoping to avoid any topic that might lead on to the subject of Father Jozsef and his crusade to save her soul.

'There was a heck of a rumpus down Meresti tonight, squad cars all over the place, cops stopping everyone for their IDs. Casey's looks like it's been ram-raided, stuff all over the place.'

Aunt Lisha sighed and shook her head.

'Abundance like want ruins many,' she declared.

A twinge of sadness touched Marta's heart. After her father died Aunt Lisha had moved in with her mother and her. Then, when the farm in Rietsa was finally sold and they had had to move to the city, Aunt Lisha had come with them. The old women's country sayings had once seemed quaint. Now, in the midst of the pandemonium that was Goval, they sounded outdated and irrelevant.

Mrs Ionescu stubbed out her cigarette in the glass ashtray.

'What do you think to our latest addition?'

Marta got up and crossed to the mahogany china cabinet standing between the windows. She cast her eye over the glass shelves, packed with clumsily crafted figurines: farmyard animals, standing and lying; a sheepdog rolling on its back; workers hoeing and lifting bales of hay. Her mother lived for her memories of Rietsa, the village where she had been born and lived for over sixty years, marrying a farmer and raising three children along the way. Marta wished that, just once in a while, the old woman would try to find some pleasure in the world she inhabited now rather than always looking back.

'Ah, the dun foal,' she said, spotting the new acquisition on the middle shelf, a tiny colt with white markings on its flank, its long legs stretched out as though it had just managed to stand up for the first time. 'He's cute.'

'Yes,' her mother said, coughing harshly. 'A real beauty, isn't he?'

Marta knelt on the rug, her face next to the glass, and inspected the colt up close.

'Where did you find him?'

'Lester's,' Aunt Lisha said. 'He called us when he came in last week.'

Marta was relieved; at least Lester's was on Meresti Street. The thought of her frail sixty-eight-year-old mother traipsing around some of the seedier junk and pawn shops away from the main drag gave her nightmares. Having the two of them living nearby was convenient from the point of view of visiting and helping out but these days she wished they could be back in the country, safe amongst the people they had grown up with. Only, of course, the Rietsa they knew had disappeared years ago.

'Lord,' Mrs Ionescu said, easing herself to her feet. 'I'd best serve this supper before it's baked to death.'

'You want a hand, Mama?'

'I'll shout you when I've dished up.'

Using the chair backs to steady herself Marta's mother made her way slowly to the kitchen. As always she shut the door behind her, an old country habit, a signal to the men and children to keep out. Marta got to her feet and returned to her place on the settee.

'She seems to be getting wobblier by the day,' she whispered to Aunt Lisha, knowing full well her mother's penchant for listening at doors.

'Age, my dear,' the old lady replied, a wistful smile passing over her wrinkled lips. 'It gets us all in the end. She's totally with it though. Hasn't got her mind yet, thank the Lord.'

'Are you coping alright? Really?'

Lisha patted her niece's thigh.

'We're fine,' she said, 'you really shouldn't worry so much.

When Ele can't walk I'll do the shopping alone. When I can't walk you can do it. Deal?'

'Deal,' Marta said, hugging her aunt. Over the old woman's shoulder she caught sight of the plain silver cross and two wood-framed photographs standing on the shelf: her mother and father on their wedding day; her two brothers – Aurel and Rica – in front of their dilapidated van, the day before they left home to look for work, three days before they died in a pile-up on the N10 near Bordeaux. The women relaxed their grip and Aunt Lisha sat back.

'Not a day goes by when she doesn't say a prayer for them,' she said.

Marta nodded slowly.

'They were good times.'

Her aunt smiled thoughtfully.

'The best.'

The old lady got to her feet and crossed to the dresser. Opening the cupboard she took out a white cotton tablecloth and a packet of crimson paper napkins and placed them on the table. This was the signal for Marta to lift the ancient, battered canteen from the dresser drawer. Then, as they did every time Marta came to eat, the two women laid the table together.

Afterwards they sat down in front of the comscreen and called up World of Puzzles™. Aunt Lisha was a great fan of the channel and spent hours every day working her way through the various word games it carried. Marta didn't share her aunt's enthusiasm – or patience – and never gave the channel a moment's thought any other time. But her affection for her father's sister, and the two women's good-natured competitiveness, made this slot a particularly enjoyable part of her visits.

Fifteen minutes later, as Marta keyed in the final clue in their second crossword, she noticed that her mother was taking even longer than usual.

'You alright in there, Mama? Need any help?'

There was no reply but, before she could move, the door opened and the trickle of mouth-watering aromas that had been seeping into the living room became a flood. Mrs Ionescu emerged triumphant, her weathered faced covered in beads of sweat.

'It's ready,' she announced, before setting out on her ritual pre-supper journey to the bathroom. Her bladder wasn't so good these days either.

Heading into the kitchen to take up her usual role as server-in-chief, Marta was surprised by the number of dishes laid out ready on the worktop. Her mother's cooking had always been a source of wonder to her; what she achieved with a few goose livers and kidneys, some wine and garlic, Marta had never been able to reproduce. But today she had excelled herself. Apart from the soup there was freshly baked bread and a bowl of steaming polenta, and, on the hob, a pan of tochitura simmering away merrily. Marta leaned forwards and inhaled the scent of sweet peppers and pork sausage.

'Mama,' she shouted. 'You really shouldn't have.'

'Nonsense,' she heard her mother's distant reply. 'Oh, and there's something special for you in the fridge.'

Marta opened the refrigerator and came face to face with a small baklava on a plate, honey oozing out from between the layers of flaky pastry: her favourite dessert. Intrigued, she walked to the kitchen door, plate in hand.

'You two on a diet?'

'Lent,' Aunt Lisha whispered, rolling her eyes. 'Don't let on to your mother you've forgotten or I'll never hear the end of it.'

'Oops, sorry… Well, it's really too much. This lot must have cost a week's pension.'

The lavatory flushed and Mrs Ionescu could be heard moving around in the bathroom.

'Hush, you idiot,' Aunt Lisha hissed. 'She's saying she loves you, the only way she knows how.'

EIGHT

The following morning Marta got up at around eight to feed Gypsy before crawling back into bed, intending to sleep for another hour or two. She emerged in the middle of the afternoon, exhausted and disorientated. Thankfully, after a long, hot shower and something to eat she started to feel human once more. Scrolling through her messages while savouring her croissant and apricot jam, she was delighted to find one from Dina: she and a few of their workmates were meeting up that evening to celebrate trainee Bela Vlas's nineteenth birthday, was Marta up for it? Marta responded straightaway, delighted at the prospect, after her recent labours, of an evening out with the girls.

Her g-mails and messages answered, Marta stretched out on the sofa and, with Gypsy purring contentedly on her lap, called up the reader on her tablet. With its sinister mafia machinations and high-octane chases, the Olaru novel kept Marta engrossed right through to the end when the bloody and battered hero revealed all to the crime-fighting judge. Glancing up at the comscreen she was amazed to find she had been reading for nearly two hours without a break. Luxury!

'TV ON,' she ordered, putting her tablet on the table. 'NEWS CHANNEL CARADEA.'

The hourly update contained brief reports on the police hunt for the perpetrators of the Union House bombing ('investigations ongoing'), the federal budget negotiations in Brussels ('discussions continuing'), and the traffic disruption in Caradea ('unlikely to improve for several days'). Miffed that there was nothing about VisionPlace's success in finding new accommodation for the UES employees, Marta was about to put the comscreen on stand-by when the continuity announcer returned:

'We cross now to Police Central, where a press conference concerning the recent bombing at Union House is about to start.'

Marta sat up, eager to learn more.

On the screen, three men and a woman were sitting behind a table covered in black cloth. Marta recognised the woman, Cathy White, one of VisionPlace's PR people, and beside her Michael Brancusi, the poor man looking sleep-deprived and haunted. Next to Mr Brancusi was a lean, silver-haired cop who looked way past retirement age and next to him, at the other end of the line, was a middle-aged guy who, with his broad shoulders and barrel chest, looked like a wrestler. Judging by all the scrambled egg and medal ribbons on the two cops' navy uniforms, they were pretty high up.

'Good morning, ladies and gentlemen,' the older policeman began, leaning towards the bouquet of microphones sprouting from the table. The assembled journalists shifted in their seats, eager to catch his opening words.

'I'm Commander Victor Litani and this is Captain Istvan Pal. Captain Pal and I are members of the Regional Anti-Terrorism Unit.'

Unfazed by the loud murmur running around the room the speaker pressed on, introducing Cathy and Michael Brancusi, before pulling a pair of gold-rimmed spectacles from his top pocket and slipping them onto his nose.

'I have a short statement to make concerning recent events at the regional government offices in Caradea. Following this Mr

Brancusi will appeal for assistance and Captain Pal and I will take questions.'

The commander opened the sheet of paper in his hands and started to read.

'On the evening of Friday March twenty-second, the UES offices at Union House in Caradea were badly damaged by an explosion. A detailed forensic examination of the scene has confirmed that the explosion was caused by an improvised explosive device. One member of staff, Mrs Sophie Brancusi, was killed in the explosion. Mrs Brancusi, a human rights lawyer who worked for various Union agencies over the past thirteen years, was forty-two years old. She is survived by her husband and one daughter. On behalf of Europol, and the Caradea Police Department, I would like to offer Mrs Brancusi's family our deepest sympathies.'

Commander Litani paused and nodded to Mr Brancusi, who leaned towards the microphones, camera flashes lighting up his face.

'Whoever planted this bomb,' Michael began, his voice quivering. He stopped and cleared his throat before continuing, '...has ripped apart... a close and loving family.'

Marta felt her eyes fill; this was excruciating TV. But when a photograph of Sophie Brancusi was flashed up on the screen behind her distraught husband, she was immediately hooked. It was the blonde, expensively dressed woman she had seen in Arpad's surveillance photos, sitting in a car with Ludmilla Fedoruk.

'...I'm appealing to anyone who knows anything at all about this... wicked act to please get in touch with the police.'

Michael sat back, drained, as more camera flashes lit up the panel. On cue, Commander Litani resumed control.

'Thank you, Mr Brancusi. I'd echo your words and appeal to anyone listening to or watching this broadcast who has any information concerning this act of terrorism to contact the Caradea Police Department on the dedicated hotline. The number is displayed on the bottom of your screen. I should add that a

54

reward is available to anyone providing the police with information leading to a conviction.'

The Commander paused, removed his spectacles and cast his eyes across the sea of faces in front of him.

'The regional government has assured me that all necessary resources will be made available to ensure that the perpetrators of this monstrous assault are found and brought to trial. Captain Pal here is taking charge of the investigation forthwith. He brings a formidable background in counter-terrorism to the task.'

Whilst his record was paraded before the assembled journalists, the camera zoomed in on the captain's face. The man's bulk and shaven head, his dark, unblinking eyes, gave Marta the impression that he was the Commander's attack dog, an impression reinforced once the questioning got underway. Picking up on his boss's confirmation that there was no clue yet as to the bombers' identity, the captain lay his heavy forearms on the table.

'The final stage of the new governmental arrangements take effect from the first of January next year,' he said gruffly. 'Those who attempt to use violence to oppose further integration will be met with the full force of the law…'

This was more than the usual good cop-bad cop routine, Marta thought, turning up the volume.

'…Whether it's the NOL or anyone else running on an anti-integration ticket, whether it's organised crime or international terror, we will respond with all the means at our disposal. We will not discount any options.'

It was a threat; the gloves were off. But Marta's mind was elsewhere. Why, she was wondering, was human rights lawyer Sophie Brancusi sitting in a car with supposed trafficker Ludmilla Fedoruk? And how did all this fit with what Arpad had told her?

*

By the time Marta arrived at the newly opened bierkeller in the Jewellery Quarter, it was clear that the place was proving to be a hit. As she started down the wooden steps she could hear Dina's piercing laughter, slicing through the crowd's shouting, singing and stomping.

'Hi, babe!' the normally reserved birthday girl Bela screeched when Marta finally reached her colleagues. 'We thought you'd stood us up!'

The five women were crowded around a tiny, round table overflowing with steins.

'Where are all the fellas?' Marta asked, sitting herself on the small wooden keg they had reserved for her. She had been looking forward to some good, innocent flirting.

'Bela scared 'em off,' Dina bawled. 'Said she was gonna snog anyone who bought her a drink!'

Dina's grotesque stein-kissing demonstration had them all creased with laughter, even the waitress who arrived to clear the table and take Marta's order. Marta loved the girl's traditional outfit: the short puffy sleeves on her white peasant blouse, the tightly laced bodice.

'God, I could do with one of those,' she announced, eyeing the girl's pronounced cleavage and cupping her own tiny breasts. 'Never found a bra yet to make something of these.'

The women screeched and tittered. Dina offered her glass to Marta.

'Here, have some of this,' she yelled. 'Keep you going until Heidi gets back.'

Seconds later the oompah band struck up again and a man in lederhosen pointed with his baton at the words rolling across the screen behind him. Everyone in the cellar started singing.

It was gone midnight when the women rolled up arm in arm at Blue, the biggest nightclub in Caradea, singing 'The Lonely Goatherd'. After all the worry of the last week – sorting the UES accommodation, wondering what to make of Arpad's revelations – Marta was loving just drinking and gossiping and being with her friends. Soon after their arrival, she and Bela hit the dancefloor and were strutting their stuff when Paolo Gheorghiu came over and started dancing with them. Marta was gobsmacked; he was usually so respectful at the club, the perfect team captain. Now here he was gyrating in front of them without a hint of shyness. She thought at first he might be using her to get to Bela, who, after all, was a good-looking girl with a fantastic figure. But Paolo barely spoke to the birthday girl; it was Marta whose ear he shouted into in between the thump, thump, thump of the music, telling her what an inspiration she was and thanking her again for the surprise party at the club, insisting that she put a bet on Dynamo to go through to the Semis.

'It's a dead cert,' he kept repeating, sounding just like his dad. 'You can't lose.'

Marta teased him about being out so late, demanded to know why he wasn't tucked up in bed getting a good night's sleep before college.

'And don't you have some kind of fitness regime to follow?' she added, wagging her finger.

Paolo took it all in his stride, shrugging off the playful gibes.

'Blue's my favourite club, I love the place. Why haven't I seen you here before, Marta?'

'Oh, I'm more a diner than a dancer,' she said. 'But it's nice to have a change sometimes.'

By now Bela had retired and was sitting with the others, staring daggers at the couple from Goval. Marta was flattered. How many good-looking eighteen-year-olds would get up in a place like this and dance with someone nearly twice their age? Having Dina there to witness it made the experience all the more sweet. And when, after a final round of arm waving and hip shaking, Paolo went off to find his mates and Marta returned to her table, it was obvious from the way she was interrogated that her street cred had soared. All of her companions recognised the would-be football star and all of them apart from Bela were impressed by her supposed ability to attract the attention of someone so young and handsome. The harder she protested – 'He's just a kid from the youth club. I've known him since he was in first grade' – the more exaggerated her friends' winks and mock outrage. Their envy was good-natured but could not be disguised. And Marta enjoyed every minute of it.

NINE

The next day Marta was woken around nine by Gypsy jumping on the duvet and nuzzling her face, chiding her for forgetting his breakfast. She crawled out of bed and stumbled into the kitchen, hungover and, having not got home until gone four, seriously sleep-deprived. After spooning some food into the cat's dish and setting it down on his mat, Marta went back to bed. The next time she came round it was gone two and she was crashed out on the sofa in her dressing gown, a chat show on the comscreen. She lay there for a while, dimly intrigued by the aggression displayed by the host towards his guests, the studio audience's willingness to applaud such boorishness.

Eventually, her tummy rumbling, her mouth parched, Marta hauled herself to her feet and went through to the kitchen. The fridge was practically empty, just a bag of lettuce, some tomatoes, a half-empty carton of milk and the remnants of a loaf of cozonac: sweet bread, her mother's trial of a new walnut recipe for Easter. Marta put the bread on a plate, sliced it into three and, with a mug of freshly brewed coffee in the other hand, returned to the living area. She would have to go to the supermarket at some point to restock but, for now, she needed to get her brain in gear.

*

Her backpack stuffed with groceries, a full carrier bag in each hand, Marta kicked the front door to behind her, switched on the lights and staggered through to the kitchen.

'Careful, boy,' she cried, as Gypsy, meowing his welcome, looped himself around her legs, threatening to upend her. Sitting the bags on the floor, the backpack on the worktop, she dropped her keys and leant down to stroke the cat.

'I know. What a bad mum I am, leaving you alone all this time.'

After putting away the shopping and feeding Gypsy, Marta called Flori Melinte. She had bought her friend a bottle of red wine as a thank-you for helping out with Paolo's celebrations and organising the clear-up after she had left. Could she drop by with it this evening?

'Sure, I'm not going anywhere,' Flori said, delighted. 'Hey. Why don't you stay for supper?'

Marta hesitated; she was tempted. Her friend was a fantastic cook and just the smell of her food could put kilos on a woman's hips.

'Come on, Bunny, a couple of hours won't hurt. Anyhow, Bianca's staying at her dad's the night, I could do with the company.'

Marta liked Flori a lot. Their shared experience of growing up in a village was the source of much banter and they both detested the endless romanticisation of a way of life that, for them, had been characterised by poverty, ignorance and archaic inequality. But still…

'I'm sorry, Flori, I promised my mum I'd call round. I've got her shopping, too.'

'So, come here after.'

'Tell you what, I'll drop the wine in tonight but let's get together next week and I'll happily eat my way through your fridge.'

'I'll hold you to that. Send me your shifts and we'll sort a date.'

*

Round at her mother's, Marta left the shopping on the side in the kitchen as instructed and made a pot of coffee. A traditional lament was playing on the radio and the two pensioners, through in the living room, were reading in companionable silence. Marta felt a warm calmness creep over her, a sense that all was well with the world. It was a feeling she experienced less frequently these days, what with her busy job, her mother's declining health, her youth club responsibilities and perplexing love life alongside all the world's woes, ever-present in the media. After giving the coffee a final stir Marta loaded the pot, mugs, spoons and sugar onto the zebra-patterned tray that had been in the family for as long as she could remember and carried the lot through to the living room.

Mrs Ionescu put down her paperback.

'Thank you, dear.'

Marta poured the coffees and placed a mug on the coaster beside her mother, just as Aunt Lisha, sitting on the sofa, her head buried in the newspaper, cried out.

'Oh, dear lord. They've found her body.'

'Whose body?' said Mrs Ionescu.

'That missing Ukranian girl,' Aunt Lisha replied, turning the paper around in order to show them the picture of Ludmilla Fedoruk.

Her hear thumping, Marta placed her aunt's coffee on the mat and glanced at the photo of the pretty blonde.

'Oh, the prostitute,' Mrs Ionescu said with a sniff.

Marta scowled at her mother.

'Don't! Just imagine how those poor women must feel. Imprisoned. Abused day and night… Does it say what happened to her, Auntie?'

'No, it doesn't… "The body was identified by Ms Fedoruk's sister…" "Cause of death is still to be determined…" Says they're doing another post-mortem on Friday.'

Mrs Ionescu screwed up her face.

'I'd castrate the lot of 'em, those traffickers.'

'They've got to catch them first, Mama. Then they've got to convince the girls they, and their families, will be safe if they testify.'

Mrs Ionescu groaned and leaned on the table as though bowed by the weight of evil in the world.

'So long as the good Lord sees fit to give me breath I'll never understand how men can be so cruel.'

An unhappy silence descended and Marta knew that she must make it her business to find out just how much Arpad knew about this poor woman and her demise.

TEN

The following morning Marta called Arpad and was amazed when he actually answered.

'Hi, hon,' he said, smiling brightly. 'How's your break going?'

'Great. I've cleaned the place up, had a wild night out with the girls and haven't had a single call from David.'

'Awesome. Wish I could be there with you. When do you go back?'

'I'm on a late tomorrow... Where are you?'

'At the architect's, going over the Welcome Home design.'

'Right. I wondered if you fancy a trip to Screen City tonight? There's a new Petrescu movie I'd like to see.'

'So I heard, it's supposed to be hilarious. What time's it on?'

'There's a show at eight-thirty. How about we meet at eight-fifteen in the foyer?'

'Hang on, let me check.'

The screen went blank briefly before Arpad reappeared.

'Sure, let's do it.'

'Great, see you there.'

*

Arpad never made it to the cinema that evening. As Marta waited for him in the foyer, eyeing the moviegoers streaming in through the huge glass doors, her irritation growing, he called and apologised.

'Something's cropped up,' he said. 'I'm running late. Can you sort out the tickets and I'll be along in time for the start?'

'But the programme begins in less than ten minutes.'

'OK, leave me a ticket at the desk and I'll meet you inside.'

Marta struggled to contain her anger.

'Don't be an arse,' she said. 'Even if you set out now you'll miss the first ten or fifteen minutes.'

'Well, let's make it another night then.'

'Forget it. Something else more important will no doubt crop up.'

'Now who's being an arse!'

Was she being an arse? She didn't think so.

'I've got to go.'

'But—'

Marta pocketed her palmcom and stood in the middle of the milling crowd unsure what to do for the best. Should she stay and watch the film? Should she call Arpad back and apologise, make alternative arrangements? Feeling too annoyed to pursue either option she left the cinema and walked down the hill to Central Terminus. So much for her night out!

*

Marta stood in the kitchen in her dressing gown, stirring biscuit into the leftover chicken stew she had emptied into Gypsy's dish. Her head ached and she was seething. She really resented Arpad's turning up, especially in the state he was in. He should have just let her be, allow her bad mood to blow over. She had actually been enjoying herself back home, clearing the backlog of club business, going through the suggestions members and volunteers had submitted for the annual outing, sending out a reminder about not opening on Good Friday. Then, just before midnight, he'd arrived, stinking of whisky, his suit all crumpled, his tie stuffed in his pocket.

'You ignored my messages,' he barked, leaning against the doorframe to steady himself. He was sweating profusely.

'Arpad, keep it down, will you? You'd better come in.'

Marta had switched off her palmcom after receiving his third message, a pathetic, slurred pleading that had rekindled the annoyance she had felt at the cinema. But as she watched him stumble across to the living area and collapse onto her stubby sofa she decided that now would not be a good time to tell him that. And it definitely wasn't the time to raise the question of what he knew about the dead Ukranian woman.

'You want a coffee?'

'What happened to that *pălincă* I left? I'll have some of that.'

His coldness upset her; he could be so rude when he was drunk.

A vigorous brushing against her calves interrupted Marta's irate reflections. Gypsy was hungry.

'Hold on,' she said grumpily, bending down to set his dish on the mat. 'Why do *you* always have to be first?'

She watched the cat bury his head in his dish then set about sorting out his litter tray.

Since the day Mrs Munteanu had handed him over, a tiny grey bundle, Gypsy had never been outside. Marta intended to keep it that way, too; she didn't want him scavenging like some unwanted stray or ending up a mangled mess by the side of the road. After washing her hands she pulled out a stool and sat down by the worktop to eat her breakfast, a bowl of Bran-U-Like drowned in milk. Seconds later she heard the bathroom door slam, followed soon afterwards by the sound of Arpad hacking in the shower.

He had had his *pălincă*, several of them in fact, whilst rambling on about how successful his meeting had been, how he still wanted to see the film, how sorry he was for messing her about. Marta had hoped that he would crash out on the sofa so she could throw a blanket over him and leave him to it. In a one-bedroomed apartment there was only one other option, and there was no way she was in the mood to share her bed. Unfortunately, he had seen things differently and, his prolonged slur of an apology over, had started to sweet-talk her. In the end, her excuses clearly provoking rather than discouraging him, she had allowed him into her bed. Soon afterwards he had rolled off her and fallen asleep and, not long after that, had started snoring, lying on his back like a sack of damp rice, unresponsive to her nudges and urgent whispers. It all made for a miserable night, his snorts and groans and farting, her fears and disappointment festering in the fusty air. No wonder she had a headache.

The bathroom door opened and Arpad sauntered out naked, rubbing his hair with a towel as he crossed to the bedroom. He paused and sniffed the air.

'That chocolate smells good,' he said, grinning.

He had a fantastic body, she couldn't deny that. All that work with the weights in his spare room paid off. He knew it too; they often joked about his vanity.

'You want some?'

'Yeah, that'd be great.'

'Anything to eat?'

'No thanks.'

He wandered off to the bedroom, leaving Marta to debate with herself whether or not to broach the subject that had been plaguing her for much of the night. Seconds later his head reappeared around the bedroom doorframe.

'Can you call me a cab for eight?'

'Sure.'

Marta felt a flash of satisfaction; at least Tony would benefit from her lousy night. Tapping her palmcom she voice-messageed

Comfy Cars then made Arpad his chocolate. The next moment her lover – how inappropriate that word sounded this morning – rushed into the kitchen in his boxer shorts and vest, trousers in hand, a cigarette between his lips.

'I don't know what the hell this is,' he said, pointing at a large orange stain on the back of one of the legs. 'Do you mind having a go at getting it out? Please?'

Marta would have liked to have told him where to stuff his stains but she didn't have the energy for a fight. Instead she sighed loudly and held out her hand. Arpad gave her the trousers and inhaled deeply on his cigarette.

'You're an angel, thanks.'

Then he was gone, leaving her with his soiled pants and a cloud of second-hand smoke. Funny, she had never minded his smoking, so long as it was not in her home.

'Arpad,' she called after him, 'would you mind putting that out, please?'

'Sorry, hon,' he shouted without turning around, tossing the cigarette into the toilet pan before disappearing once more into the bedroom.

Marta picked up the trousers and went over to the sink. As she stood there sponging the stain she gazed out through the net curtains at the empty playground opposite, her annoyance fuelled by the sounds of a bass box booming somewhere, the old couple in the apartment below rowing.

'Love is blind,' she heard her mother say. 'But marriage finds its cure.'

*

After Arpad left, Marta couldn't settle to anything. She felt tired and angry, disgusted with him and with herself for giving in to him. Going in to work proved a welcome diversion, getting her out of the apartment and forcing her to focus on matters unrelated to her personal troubles: the backlog of mails and messages that had accumulated whilst she'd been away, a briefing from David on the progress of the Union House relocation, two housing complaints requiring her urgent attention. And (of course) a water-cooler update from Dina on her lastest toyboy. But when, towards the end of her shift, Arpad messaged Marta, apologising for letting her down and for his behaviour, her anger swelled once more. Determined not to reply, she spent the last hour at work trying to do her job while brooding on her growing disenchantment with her and Arpad's relationship. Back home, exhausted, she had a surprisingly good night's sleep but then, early the next morning while she was eating her breakfast, a message arrived.

'How about coming over to my place tonight and watching the match? We can order something in to eat, it'll be like the old days.'

Marta felt insulted.

'What sort of an offer is that?' she complained to Dina, sitting on the tram out to Jacquira. 'Watching a football match, for Christ's sake.'

Her friend told her to look on the bright side.

'If it was a choice between watching the Platinum League quarter-finals and spending time with me, most men I know would say it's a no-brainer!'

Marta laughed at her friend's unending ability to weave her love life into every conversation. Then she remembered what Paolo had said when they had met at Blue, his insistence that she place a bet on Dynamo. A little flutter might be fun!

Come lunchtime Marta found a seat by the lake and called Arpad. She told him straight: she didn't like it when he got so drunk; he changed into a stranger, rude and nasty. If she did come over he must promise to go easy on the booze. When she had finished her haranguing he gave her a sheepish grin and shrugged his shoulders.

'OK, hon, I promise.'

Seeing the look on his face she felt for him. For once he seemed genuinely sorry.

'Alright. I'll come.'

'Great, I'll send you a cab. Is six OK?'

She did not protest. The taxi would save her money and, anyway, he owed her big time!

Later that afternoon, on her way home from work, Marta did something she had never done before in her life: entered a betting shop (on Meresti) and placed a bet (twenty Euros on Dynamo making it through to the semis). Feeling strangely emboldened by this simple act, a little over two hours later, soon after she had sat down in Arpad's living room and tasted the red wine he had poured them both, she asked the question she had been dying to ask since Aunt Lisha had made her dramatic announcement.

'So what happened to Ludmilla Fedoruk?'

Arpad gave Marta that look, the one that usually accompanied his 'let's not talk about work now' fudges. But this time, sensing her determination, he quickly backed down.

'I guess her associates caught up with her before we did,' he told her. 'The woman had become a liability. They got rid of her.'

Arpad's obvious contempt for the woman he and his colleagues were supposedly hunting left Marta cold. Whatever her crimes she didn't deserve to end up in a ditch in the middle of nowhere with her throat cut, her body covered in cigarette burns. Marta could have pressed on, asked for more detail, but there was nothing to be gained. Ludmilla Fedoruk was dead and there was no way she could verify whatever Arpad chose to tell her. So she sat back and watched the match which, thankfully, turned out to be hugely entertaining. Dynamo landed a miracle win against FC Kiev –

three-one, taking them through to the semi-finals – yielding Marta nearly three hundred Euros. Sadly, her euphoria evaporated soon after the match had ended, despite Arpad's best efforts.

'It's a great shame young Gheorghiu never took up my offer,' he said, handing her a glass of celebratory champagne. 'Yes, I could have made him his fortune by the time he was twenty.'

'You mean, he could have made you yours!'

'Ha, you've seen through me.'

And she had, she really had. Later, when they made love, she was barely present, dreaming of other places and other faces, feeling no more than some faint echoes of whatever it was they had once shared.

ELEVEN

Within a quarter hour of arriving at Flori Melinte's place and uncorking the wine she had dropped off the previous week, Marta was transported to Flori's turbulent world, with its bloody-minded ex and quarrelsome teenage kids. But once her friend had let off steam, and the two of them had imbibed a couple of glasses of wine, the conversation moved quickly on to more agreeable topics. Sitting at the dining table in the Melintes' pokey living room, relishing her friend's heavenly stuffed peppers, Marta felt blessed to have someone amongst the volunteers who thought about the bigger picture, about the things that so often vexed her, like the club's policies and marketing and the annual club outing.

'I've found three hotels on the coast that offer discounts for groups,' Flori revealed enthusiastically. 'As long as they're properly supervised. An' I found a place that does outward bound for kids, too. Cheap. They'd love it, Marta, tramping over the hills.'

Marta told her friend about the other suggestions she had received, including music-making workshops in an Eastern Orthodox monastery in Moldavia and a week helping down-and-outs in Bucharest. Flori definitely wasn't keen on the latter.

'Nah, I don't think so,' she said, shaking her head. 'One, I doubt the kids'd go for it. Two, Goval's got enough alcoholics and addicts of its own. An' anyhow, would *you* want to give up a week of *your* school holiday or annual break for such a depressing job? Think about it.'

The conversation rolled on, fuelled by Flori's delicious mititei, grilled to a T, and a second bottle of red. Money was the primary concern, of course. With only a modest annual stipend from the city council and a small and shrinking pot of regular donations from a few local businesses, the club's financial resources were stretched. But factors other than money would play an important part in the final decision and its execution. The staff who ran the club were all volunteers, including Marta, and support for whatever option she finally recommended would rely not only on the members' buy-in but on that of the adults, too. One thing Marta and Flori were completely aligned on, though, were the benefits to be had. Many of the club's regular attendees were kids from families that couldn't afford an annual holiday or who, for economic or social reasons, rarely travelled outside Caradea. Witnessing the delight on the kids' faces, the impact on their self-confidence and sociability of spending just a week canoeing down rivers or hiking in the mountains, was priceless and something that drove them both on.

After dinner the two women stretched out on the sofa, sated, to watch the local news on Flori's decrepit minicom, coffees to hand. The lead item was the latest police statement concerning the ongoing investigation into the Union House bombing, delivered by the bulldog-like cop Marta had seen at the previous week's press conference, standing at a podium before a room full of reporters.

'Shit, I wouldn't want to meet him down a dark alley,' Flori said with a laugh.

'…a number of lines of inquiry,' Captain Pal read in that gruff, deadpan voice. 'As yet, there are no firm leads. Further, I can confirm that no individual or group has claimed responsibility for the bombing.'

Flori, as always, was determined to comment on every bit of news.

'Nearly two weeks and they've found nothing? It's pathetic!'

The bulldog was not taking questions and turned abruptly to leave the room. Flori rolled her eyes.

'I guess there's—'

Marta abruptly raised her hand as a photograph of Sophie Brancusi flashed up on the screen.

'Sorry, it was her funeral today. I want to hear this.'

They watched in silence as the cortege was shown arriving in the rain at the City Crematorium, the hearse crawling through a sea of umbrellas. Long lenses showed the mourners stepping from their cars outside the chapel, the striking-looking teenager Marta had seen beneath the skylight taking up position at the rear of the hearse beside her father, his face pale and gaunt, his suit hanging limply from his grief-laden shoulders.

'God,' Flori said, pulled a paper handkerchief from the sleeve of her cardigan. 'That's got to be her daughter. An' what about him, poor devil, he looks like he could do with a few good meals!'

Flori sniffed and wiped her eyes.

'If it rains during a funeral,' she said, 'it means the deceased's sad... an' didn't want to die.'

The two women exchanged a puzzled look.

'Where did you drag that one up from?' Marta asked.

'It's what my gran used to say.'

Marta burst out laughing.

'Oh, Flori, you crack me up. You can take the girl out of the country, eh!'

Flori blew her nose and tucked her handkerchief away.

'Takes one to know one!' she quipped and they were off again, their laughter an antidote to the sadness in the air.

Later, a preoccupied Marta headed home along the path between the two blocks, making sure to stay in the light and keep her hand on the StunMaster inside her bag. Back safely in her apartment she kissed Gypsy goodnight and got ready for bed, unable to shift the images that had been flitting in and out of her mind since she watched the funeral on the news: her brothers' cold bodies on display in the family's kitchen, a tractor towing a trailer bearing two coffins along a dusty country lane, a procession of mourners following behind led by her grieving mum and dad. Right now Marta's memories of that bleak day overshadowed everything.

TWELVE

Marta's visit to Natalia High had gone well. After completing a repair assessment in the senior girls' lavatories she had returned to the offices and run through the annual maintenance schedule with the Facilities Manager. After a brief chat, and having requested just two minor amendments, he had happily signed off the document. Emerging from the school's administration block into the sunshine, Marta headed down the driveway leading to the main gate, delighted with a job well done. She would be back in Jacquira in time for lunch with Dina, too. A bonus. Ahead of her, sitting on a bench beside the drive, beneath a large oak tree, a man was gazing at his palmcom. There was something familiar about the lonely, angular figure – those long thin legs, the unruly black hair – and, as she neared, she realised that it was Michael Brancusi, whose wife's funeral she and Flori had watched just last week. Her immediate thought was to walk straight past and avoid disturbing the poor fellow. But he looked so pitiful sitting there all alone and she decided to slow down.

'Hello. It's Mr Brancusi, isn't it?'

The man raised his head and she saw a terrible weariness in his eyes. It was a look she had seen before, on the faces of kids or parents whose lives had been shattered by drugs or crime or chronic disease, on people who had neared the end of their tether.

'I'm sorry, have we met?'

'Marta Ionescu, VisionPlace. I came to look at your skylight.'

'Of course,' he said, slipping his palmcom into his pocket. 'I remember now.'

'Do you mind if I sit down?'

Michael shook his head and Marta sat. It was a pleasant spot, out of the glare of the sun.

'Is your skylight OK now?'

'The…? Oh yes, thanks, it's been fine.'

They lapsed into silence, interrupted only by the sound of a bee humming around the tree's lower branches.

'I saw your wife's funeral on TV,' Marta said. 'All those people outside the crem… She must have been a wonderful person.'

Michael nodded, forlorn.

'What year are your kids in?' he asked.

'Oh, I don't have any kids, my company's got the contract to maintain this place. I was here to assess some repairs, a spot of petty vandalism in the girls' toilets.'

The man shook his head.

'They can be monsters, can't they?'

'Ha! Tell me about it. I run a youth club.'

'Really? You must be a glutton for punishment.'

'I dunno, I suppose it's a bit like being a grandparent. At least I can hand them back. And it's only once a week.'

Michael gave Marta an odd look, as though he was trying to weigh her up.

'So how did you get into that?'

'Through our local church originally. Then I fell out with the priest – well, with religion, really – and set up my own group a few years back. I still hire the local hall but it's not a church group as such, however much the priest likes to think so.'

Marta recalled the girl staring up at her through the skylight, her sad expression.

'Is your daughter a student here?'

Michael turned and cast her a doleful look.

'Yes… Year Ten.'

Marta stayed silent. Given everything the man must have been through she did not want to appear pushy.

'The Principal called us in,' Michael continued at length, staring at the ground. 'Steffi's been skipping lessons. I'm afraid the meeting didn't go very well.'

Marta got the impression that Michael was not used to dealing with kids. Perhaps his wife looked after that side of things.

'I'm sorry. Do you have any other children?'

'No,' he replied, with an air of resignation. 'We never got round to it.'

Marta recognised the scenario, the small professional family, both parents working long hours, their kids bought off with money and presents. It was so different from Goval, with its high unemployment and sprawling families, people always on the move, searching for work. They sat awhile like old friends, comfortable in their silence.

'Well, I'd better head off,' Marta said, getting to her feet. 'I've got a report to finish this afternoon. It was nice to meet you again, Mr Brancusi. I hope things, you know, get back on track for you and your daughter.'

'Thank you. I hope so too.'

Marta carried on down the driveway. When she reached the gate she looked back to see Michael sitting on that lonely bench, gazing at his palmcom once more.

THIRTEEN

Marta sat in the back of the taxi going over her reasoning, reassuring herself once more that she was making the right decision. Giving Arpad his marching orders was not the result of any single incident but, rather, the accumulated impact of a host of slights and irritations. His erratic working hours and increasingly heavy drinking. The bizarre revelations concerning his supposed undercover work. The standing her up, yet again, and turning up at her place uninvited. And drunk. Etcetera, etcetera… Until quite recently she had believed that she could turn things around, recapture the excitement of her and Arpad's first year together. But the last few weeks had convinced her otherwise. He wouldn't like her turning up like this, of course, unannounced. She had learned early on in their time together that he did not like surprises. But, heh, tough shit…

The taxi pulled up beside the entrance to a dark alleyway and Marta could see, half way along, the pale glow of the neon arrow pointing down to Adrian's basement bar. This was Arpad's territory, the place he had brought her the day after they had first made love, where they had sat side by side in their booth and exchanged sweet confidences while the smartly dressed office workers around them chatted over their lunches. Since then she had been here on many occasions, usually in the evenings when the bar's kitchen was closed and a small band of locals, mostly single and divorced businessmen who could afford Ticha's juicy rents, shared a smoky, coarse camaraderie.

After slipping her fare through the payment tray Marta paused to allow three drunks to stagger by, their arms around each other's shoulders like Russian dancers. When they had passed she said goodnight to the driver, stepped out of the cab and started down the alley. Her heart was pounding against her ribcage and her skin felt sticky beneath her flimsy blouse. This was it, time to plough under, as her father used to say. Her relationship with Arpad had run its course, she had to move on. At the foot of the concrete steps Marta paused and took a deep breath before brushing aside the bead curtain and stepping through the doorway.

'Hey,' Jotti's voice rang out from behind the counter. 'Look what the wind's blown in.'

The barman's warm greeting reassured Marta as she crossed to the bar and a dozen pairs of eyes turned to inspect her. Some faces she recognised: Wal Corbett, manager of the Porshe dealership on Pangora, Gem Pedersen, the building's caretaker, Shahi and Betta, two ageing prostitutes who regularly dropped by in between stints. Arpad was sitting at a table in the far corner with Danny French, the Englishman, and two men she didn't recognise. He looked up at her briefly, then, without reacting, lowered his eyes to inspect the playing cards in his hand.

'How are *you*, Princess?' Jotti asked, adopting the faux-camp tone he reserved for favoured female customers.

'I'm good, thanks,' Marta replied, hoping the tension wouldn't show in her voice.

'So, what can I get you tonight, my darling, the usual?'

'Why not?'

Jotti sat his cigarette in the tin ashtray and bent down to retrieve a bottle from the refrigerator. He emerged with an unopened Francusa, Marta's favourite, which he uncorked deftly before filling the glass he had taken from the shelf.

'There you go. Noroc.'

'Cheers.'

As Marta raised the glass of to her lips Jotti leaned over to stub out his cigarette.

'Watch out,' he whispered, 'he's in a *filthy* mood. Lost a lot of money.'

Marta grinned to camouflage her response.

'I guessed as much. Thanks for the warning.'

Picking up her glass she headed towards the card players' table. Seeing her approach, Arpad placed his cards face down on the table. The other men followed suit.

'Ha, Marta! Still drinking that bull's piss I see.'

She recognised the signals: the flushed face and drooping eyelids, the dishevelled hair, the desire to belittle her in front of his mates.

'Danny,' she said, pulling a chair out from under the table. 'Are you well?'

'So-so, Marta, you know how it is.'

Sitting down, she placed her glass beside the heap of fifty-Euro notes and assorted coins in the centre of the table.

'Aren't you going to introduce me to your friends, Arpad?' she asked, smiling at the two strangers.

Her soon-to-be-ex took a swig of his beer and drew deep on his cigarette.

'Marta, this is Nicholae...'

The pasty-faced man seated across from Arpad, whose jowls hung over his unbuttoned shirt collar, nodded stiffly.

'...and this is his brother, Theo.'

'Miss,' the second man said, the moustache on his bony face twitching like a nervous bird. 'I am most delighted to make your acquaintance.'

'It's a pleasure to meet you,' Marta cooed, before adding, as she felt Arpad's eyes boring into her, 'But please don't let me interrupt your game. I'll go and keep Jotti company for a while.'

Back at the bar Marta sat down on one of the tall wooden barstools and lay a twenty on the counter. In the state he was in, Arpad would be extra pissed off with her for turning up unexpectedly like this. She would need to be careful. That said, it certainly made her job easier; he wasn't exactly endearing himself to her. She swallowed her wine and placed the empty glass back on the counter. Jotti refilled it and put the note in the till.

'Not too good, eh?'

'No, not too good.'

She sipped her wine and watched Jotti washing ashtrays and polishing glasses. He was a great guy, big and generous and funny. His stories always made her laugh. When he was done at the sink he poured himself a beer, came around to the front of the counter and sat down beside her. Sure enough he was soon talking about the army.

'Did I tell you the one about smuggling the tanker full of vodka over from Ukraine?'

Marta laughed as she recalled the ridiculous tale she had heard countless times. She had hated her national service; all she seemed to do for two years was ferry officers between army bases and, on the longer drives, fight them off. But Jotti appeared to have had a great time, getting involved in numerous scams whilst serving in the Peace Corps in Bosnia and with the Union's Eastern Border Guard.

'...and then this platoon of Italian commandos opened fire at us. They thought we were the traffickers! Ha, ha, ha.'

Judging by the curses coming from the card table Arpad's luck was not improving any. Then Marta heard his raised voice, a chair scraped loudly across the floor, and she swivelled round to see him standing up and pulling on his crumpled jacket. Nicholae and Theo, still in their seats, continued to remonstrate.

'I said I'm out!'

Danny was trying to make light of the situation.

'It's no use,' he kept repeating. 'If he says he's out, then that's it.'

Marta watched Arpad moving towards her and realised just how much her feelings for him had changed. Once she had admired this man, had even been a little in awe of him. But all she saw now was a dishevelled waster, someone fast giving up on himself.

'Hiya,' Jotti said. 'Howd'ya finish up then?'

'You don't want to know, my friend. Give me another beer, eh?'

As Jotti got up to go behind the bar Arpad leaned forward and kissed Marta on the cheek. The stench of beer, cigarettes and sweat was overpowering.

'Sorry to keep you waiting, hon. Believe me… I had to see that through.'

'They don't seem to be thanking you for it,' Marta said, eyeing Danny's placatory gestures, the brothers' hunched mutterings.

'They think I've got more to burn, but I haven't. I'm all out.'

He sounded it, too, Marta thought. He must have been here most of the afternoon.

'Let's go and sit over there,' he said, nodding at an empty table by the wall, beneath a poster of the Old City. He picked up the beer bottle that Jotti had placed on the counter and led the way, mumbling as he passed the other drinkers. They sat down opposite one another and Arpad poured his beer slowly and with a great deal of concentration. Was he playing for time? Marta wondered. Did he suspect what was on her mind?

'So, you had a good day?'

Marta thought about his question. Should she respond or just get on and tell him?

'Not bad. To be honest, after the Union House rush it all feels a bit flat.'

She looked at his hands. Quite small, really, smooth-skinned. Arpad was no manual labourer, but she had seen him knock down a man a head taller than himself who had once barged into her in the street. He had never hit her, though, or even threatened to. So why did she get the feeling when he was like this that he might harm her in some way? Arpad smiled feebly and looked down at the contents of his glass.

'I could do with a shower. You want to come to my place?'

Marta did not like being put on the spot like this, she wanted some answers before she finally pulled the plug.

'What's going on, Arpad?'

'What do you mean?'

'Well, seems to me over the last few months you've been kind of… erratic, like you're letting things slip.'

Seeing the frown on his face, her anxiety leapt. The courage that had carried her here was fading fast.

'Letting what things slip?'

'Yourself, your pride. Us. When you got the Welcome Homes contract, everything was rosy. Now here you are back on the pop big time.'

He stared at her, his gaze unfathomable. Was he even drunker than he sounded? Had he taken in what she had said?

'I don't want to discuss this here,' he said, his voice low and moody. 'Why don't we go and get something to eat?'

The very idea appalled her.

'No, I don't want to eat. Thank you. We need to talk, Arpad. Now.'

'I told you, I—'

'I've been thinking… Perhaps we'd be better off having a break.'

The expression that swept across his face shocked her, a combination of rage and loathing. Then it was gone, though not before his hand had shot snake-like across the table and grabbed hers. He leaned forward as though examining his drink, peered up at her through narrowed eyes.

'Listen, bitch,' he hissed. '*You* don't finish with me. *I* finish with you.'

Then he smiled and dug his nails into her skin. Marta, horrified, felt his spittle on her face, a terrible thumping starting up inside her head. Biting her lip she tried to gather her thoughts, regretted the fact that she had sat with her back to the room, her body a screen.

'Arpad, you're hurting me,' she said quietly. 'Please stop.'

But Arpad responded by tightening his grip further. Paralysed, Marta heard Betta complaining to Shahi about her varicose veins, Gem telling a filthy joke.

'You understand me, bitch? You're mine. I call, you run.'

She wanted to cry out but was petrified of what Arpad would do if she opened her mouth.

'Look, Arpad, I'm not making you happy, not like I used to.'

'You don't get it, do you? You're my fuck, that's all there is to it.'

He wasn't saying these things to her; the man with the gorgeous suits and manicured nails and lovely manners would never talk to her like this.

'But we had something else, Arpad, something more than… that.'

'You might have done. But nothing's changed s'far as—'

Jotti had appeared beside them, Marta's bottle wrapped in a white linen napkin.

'Sorry, Marta,' he said cheerily. 'Didn't notice you were empty.'

Arpad relaxed his grip, allowing Marta to snatch her hand away.

'Thanks, Jotti,' she said, massaging her gouged flesh beneath the table top.

'You're welcome. You alright for the moment, Arpad?'

Arpad's unblinking eyes stared into Marta's.

'Yeah, I'm fine.'

Jotti lingered.

'Anything else I can get you, folks? Nibbles, a sandwich, maybe?'

Arpad looked up at Jotti and grinned before winking conspiratorially.

'Piss off, Jot. Can't you see me and Marta are busy?'

'Oh, so-o sorry. Just shout if you want anything.'

Jotti returned to the bar, taking Marta's hopes of an escape with him. She watched as Arpad lifted the bottle slowly to his wet lips and gulped down the remaining contents. He paused to wave to someone behind her.

'Bye, girls,' he shouted.

She turned to see the two tarts straightening their tiny skirts and pulling on their jackets.

'Bye, Arpad, bye, Marta,' they cried as they clomped across the room in their ridiculously high heels.

Marta waved glumly as her two potential allies deserted her, then turned back to face Arpad.

'Now listen, Marta, there's something you should know. If you try anything like that again your employers will be getting wind of your naughty ways.'

Marta wondered what on earth he was talking about. Was it her politics? They used to discuss them a lot when they first got together; he knew all about her marching with the Greens. It occurred to her that perhaps Arpad had had a breakdown, that whatever had been worrying him had finally pushed him over the edge. But she said nothing, terrified of upsetting him further.

'You never knew you were the star of some very juicy movies, did you? Very popular with the lads, I must say.'

She saw the two of them naked, cavorting on his bed.

'You bastard...' she cried, slumping back in her chair. 'Tell me you're kidding.'

Arpad's voice dropped to almost a whisper.

'Listen, I'm not going to piss about. If you're not prepared to play ball then one or two extracts from my personal movie collection will find their way onto the grid. How would your dear old mum feel about seeing her precious daughter sucking dick, eh?'

Marta's right hand landed flat on his cheek with a loud crack.

'Don't you dare bring her into this, you bastard.'

Arpad jerked back, feeling his cheek as he started to get to his feet. Marta braced herself for retaliation. But Jotti was over in a moment, his large frame towering over the two of them. Arpad slowly lowered himself back into his seat.

'Sorry, folks,' the young man said, 'you'll have to go, you know the rules. Can I call you a cab, Marta?'

Arpad raised his palms skywards and shrugged his shoulders...

'It's OK, Jot. Lovers' tiff.'

...Then fixed his eyes on Marta, a silent threat.

'We're off,' he persisted. 'Don't worry, Marta's coming with me. Isn't that right, babe?'

Marta held Arpad's stare. She despised what she saw in his eyes and she despised her own weakness and fear. Then she heard her father's voice once more and knew what she had to do: '*Don't ever back down to the bully boys, they'll never let up.*'

Had Arpad really filmed them? Would he carry out his threat? She looked up at Jotti.

'Please, Jot. A taxi would be good.'

She felt her legs shaking.

'You'll regret this, Marta,' her tormentor whispered as she got up from the table.

*

Marta had witnessed plenty of violence in her life – soldiers settling scores behind the latrines, cops beating protesters with their batons and shields – but she had never felt so frightened, so vulnerable as she had sitting opposite Arpad that evening, staring into his cold, unblinking eyes whilst his nails raked her skin. Back home she had lain in bed with the StunMaster on the bedside table and Gypsy curled up beside her, trying to fathom out how the man who had once treated her so tenderly could have behaved like that. By the time the alarm woke her and she stumbled to the shower, Marta had managed barely two hours' sleep.

Work that day was mind-numbingly boring, taken up almost entirely with the completion of detailed claims for federal compensation. March's high winds and severe flooding had delayed several of the company's infrastructure projects and, as lead support on three school refurbishments, all covered by the Union's *Force Majeure* insurance, it was Marta's job to insert the numbers on a host of online forms before forwarding these to Finance to be signed off and sent on to Brussels. The complexity of the forms – the number of ridiculous questions asked, the extent of detail required – infuriated Marta. It was bureaucracy gone mad.

At lunchtime she went for a swim, but her heart wasn't in it and she abandoned the pool after completing just three lengths. Once showered and dressed she headed for the restaurant, intending to eat her salad and check her post. But en route her palmcom double-pinged – 'Unregistered device, sender unknown' – and, although the mail was malware-free, given the threats Arpad had made the previous evening she decided to find a quiet spot in the nearest touchdown zone before opening it.

'Marta. Looks like your having fun! PS theres plenty more where this came from!'

The photograph beneath the bald, unsigned sentence was poorly lit and hard to make out. But once Marta, her heart pounding, magnified the scene there was no mistaking the identity of the naked woman sprawled across that familiar bed.

*

It was late evening by the time she summoned up the courage to call him.

'Hi, Marta, good to see you.'

His face was smooth; he had recently shaved. He had a shirt and tie on, too.

'Why did you do it, Arpad, why did you take those photos?'

'Photos? What photos?'

The image was steady; he must be sitting at his desk.

'You know damn well what photos I mean.'

'I can assure you, *I* haven't taken any photographs.'

Was he in public, was someone listening to their conversation? Was he making sure there was no evidence in case… In case what?

'Oh, come off it! You're the only person I've slept with over the last two years.'

'Marta, you're obviously distressed. You're looking tired, you should take a break.'

'Don't patronise me, you know exactly what I'm talking about.'

He didn't flinch, just kept on gazing at her, that serene half-smile on his lips.

'I'm sorry, I'd hoped the next time we spoke there might be chance of us getting things back on an even keel again.'

'I—'

'Hearing you now, though, I'm not sure you're thinking straight. Perhaps we can talk when you're feeling a bit better.'

'Fuck off, Arpad, I am never, ever going to change my mind.'

Marta jabbed her palmcom and let out an almighty scream.

*

The more Marta thought about Arpad's ridiculous and offensive denial, the greater her sense of grievance. Her affection and trust had been grossly abused; she could not to allow him to get away with what he had done. It was not as though she was some green kid, fresh from the country. She'd had a tough upbringing and her fair share of men; she knew how to handle herself. But what could she actually do? Even if she swallowed her pride and went to the cops, they would simply tell her that no crime had been committed, that the grid was full of stuff like this. And anyhow, it came via an unregistered device, what evidence did she have that Mr Radics was the sender? Calling Arpad back and appealing to his better nature was another non-starter. Why should he back down now, with all the cards in his hand? God, what a fool she'd been to ignore all the signs, to sit back and hope for the best like all the other losers at work...

'You OK, Marta?' Tony asked, his eyes connecting with hers via the rear-view mirror. 'Something bugging you?'

'I'm fine. Just got a lot of thinking to do.'

She watched Tony's lumpy, shaven head move back and forth.

'It's gotta be a guy. Am I right?'

'Something like that.'

He tutted.

'Always the way. You ladies get so involved, just not built like us fellas.'

Marta ignored Tony's prattling and gazed out at Jump City. A large fire had been lit at the edge of the shantytown and, as the cab slowed, she could see the grimy, careworn faces of the homeless in the light of the flames, the absence of hope in their eyes. Things could be worse, she told herself, much worse. Not so, her logical self countered: you have no brothers to call on, no male friends capable of exacting revenge on your behalf. You're heading for a showdown with no leverage at all. This was not entirely true, she decided: she had her father's teachings to draw on, the wisdom of a man who had successfully opposed the village council's tyranny for forty years. And she had already learned one good lesson: never again would she allow herself to be caught alone with that snake Arpad Radics.

Adrian's was much quieter than she had anticipated for a Saturday night. Aside from Jotti, perched on a high stool at the bar flicking through his newspaper, there were just three customers, Gem, Shahi and Betta, seated round a table at the back of the room.

Marta gave the trio a wave before lifting herself onto the stool beside Jotti. She was relieved that her favourite barman was working; if the worst came to the worst she was sure he would stick up for her.

'Hello, Princess,' he said. 'I didn't expect to see you back so soon.'

'That makes two of us.'

'Usual?'

'Please.'

Jotti went round behind the bar and Marta leaned closer.

'I've never seen Gem even acknowledge the girls before,' she murmured. 'What's going on?'

The barman placed a large glass in front of her and proceeded to fill it with the familiar pale yellow wine.

'Business is always slack in the run-up to Easter; perhaps he's trying to wangle himself a cut-price deal. Two for one, maybe?'

'You bad boy.'

'Times are hard, Marta,' he said, winking. 'We've all got to make the most of things.'

Marta suddenly felt confused; was Jotti coming on to her? Shrugging off the thought she asked if Arpad had been in.

'No, I've not seen him. He could have been in at lunchtime, before I arrived. But if he comes then he usually stays all afternoon… You two made up yet?'

Marta sipped the deliciously cool, dry wine. However comfortable she felt with this young man she wasn't about to share her bedroom secrets with him.

'All good things come to an end, I guess.'

The barman came back round and sat down beside her.

'Aw, that's a shame,' he said, taking a cigarette from his pack and lighting it. 'Look, I don't know what's going on between you two but just be careful. I've seen what Arpad can be like when you're *not* around.'

'I can imagine. Anyway, here's to unfinished business. Noroc.'

The barman studied her face before raising his glass.

'Noroc.'

Marta stayed in the bar for several hours, determined to see things through. As time passed a few of the regulars like Danny and Wal drifted in but when she approached them they claimed to have no idea where Arpad might be. If pressed, they quickly became agitated. It was as though they were scared or had been threatened. Or maybe they were just protecting one of their own from a supposedly irate ex. Men like these must have a routine for such situations, she imagined; she had seen a string of women on their arms over time.

Around half-ten she took herself off to the ladies' and sat in the cubicle dictating a voice message, telling Arpad that she was still in the bar and repeating the fact that she wanted to see him. But, as with the other messages she had sent – before setting out, in the taxi – this one prompted no response. The bastard was trying to make her sweat. Her anger rekindled, she headed back to the bar, weighing up as she went whether or not to march over to his apartment and buzz on the entry phone until he came down and heard her out. But she soon rejected that idea: his side street was poorly lit and quiet, and turning up there alone would only expose her to further danger. No, the bar was the safest place for her, she decided, hoisting herself back onto her chair.

Fortunately for her Jotti was on hand to keep her company, to dispense the wine and share his stories. After several more glasses she even tried one of his cigarettes but, as with all her previous efforts over the years, managed no more than a couple of half-hearted puffs before giving up… Soon after that she asked Jotti to call her a taxi. When it arrived she was surprised to find the dishy barman helping her up the steps and along the entry. The last thing she remembered was him clipping her seatbelt in place, but after that nothing, until she came round to find the taxi driver leaning in through the rear door and shaking her roughly:

'Heh, Miss, wake up. We're in Goval, you're home.'

FOURTEEN

The next day Marta was off and slept in, only stirring when she could no longer stand Gypsy's furious nuzzling. Having fed the cat she sat on a stool in the kitchen, watching a story about a green dragon on children's TV and drinking glass after glass of water to ease her sore head. When Dina called she was shocked to hear that Marta had spent the previous evening at Adrian's.

'You what?' she shouted, her mouth agape.

'I had to do something, I can't just sit around waiting for whatever it is he's got planned for me.'

'That's crazy, the psycho could have killed you... So what happened?'

'Nothing, he didn't show.'

Dina's expression softened.

'How's the hand?'

Marta held her left hand up to the palmcom so that her friend could see the angry purple bruises on the back of her hand.

'Jesus. You want to get that seen to, he could have rabies.'

'It's no joke,' Marta huffs. 'I can still feel the bastard's nails!'

'What a fucking shit. Listen, tell me you're not going to do anything stupid today.'

'Don't worry, I'm going to my mum's. Her Palm Sunday readings'll fill my heart with love, no doubt. Besides, I've got tons of washing to sort out.'

'Well, you take care. And remember, there's a bed here whenever you need it.'

'Thanks, D, you're a mate. I'll see you tomorrow.'

'OK, bye.'

Marta ended the call and returned to the story of the green dragon. But the programme's lazy spell had been broken and she found herself thinking instead about Dina's call and how grateful she was for her friend's concern and endless good humour. The idea of staying with her for a few days appealed, but Marta knew she valued her independence too much to take up the offer just yet. And anyway, Gypsy needed to be fed, his tray changed daily. He depended on her.

When her palmcom buzzed again Marta flicked open the screen half expecting it to be Dina with some piece of gossip she had forgotten to share. But all she found was a stark, anonymous message:

'Check your g-mail.'

Marta's heart sank. She had convinced herself that she had shown Arpad she was no walkover; now it looked like she had been kidding herself. But when, to be safe, she sat down on the sofa and logged onto her grid account on the comscreen, she was perplexed; the only new mails in her inbox were from people she knew – helpers at the club, friends, her mother. She eventually found the mail in the quarantine box, sender-less and with a weird address that suggested it had not come from any regular cyber-café:

'Hi, Marta. What a popular girl you are! Click on the link to see just how popular.'

Marta stared at the message. Her GSP would detect and neutralise any malicious software so she felt confident that, had Arpad booby-trapped the link, she would be protected. That said, clicking on it would be tantamount to admitting that he was getting under her skin, that he could disturb her peace of mind any time he wanted… Her pulse racing, her mouth bone dry, Marta clicked on the link.

It was her face, of course, there was no doubt about that. But the photograph on the screen appeared unreal somehow and it took a moment or two for Marta to work out why that was. The hazel eyes were hers, for sure, the smile too. But the wrinkles around her eyes had been airbrushed and her lips were fuller, as though they had been botoxed. They were also covered in pink lipstick, a colour she hated and would never use. Lowering her eyes she read the message at the foot of the screen.

'Welcome to my site, I hope you like what you see inside. But, be warned, I'm a grown-up girl with a grown-up girl's appetites. What I get up to is not for the squeamish nor, of course, for the eyes of anyone under the age of sixteen. Love, Marta.'

Her heart sank; she felt sick at the thought of what might be in store for her. But there was no way she could turn back now; there was little to be gained by burying her head in the sand. Bracing herself, she tapped 'Enter'. Immediately her photograph and the message disappeared, leaving a cartoon crimson curtain filling the screen. Corny music started up, a kind of coarse burlesque, all slippery trombones and farting trumpets, and the curtain opened slowly to show a large bed in the middle of a completely white, featureless studio, on it a group of three naked, paunchy men pawing and licking and fucking a skinny woman. At first her mind didn't comprehend what her role was in this sick game. What she was meant to be, some kind of voyeur, a cyber-madame? But when the woman turned towards the camera and smiled lasciviously Marta froze. It was her own face in the middle of that jumble of arms and cocks and backsides, her own lips emitting urgent groans amidst all the grunts and bellows. But how could this be? She had never done anything like this, had never had sex with one stranger, let alone three. As she scrutinised the grotesque creation for obvious signs of pasting and retouching a message flashed across the screen:

'Keep watching – there's plenty more here for you to enjoy.'

*

Early the next morning, bristling with fury and determination, Marta caught the bus to Red Way, a shopping mall on the far side of Goval. The district she was heading for was notoriously rough and, despite the money spent on it, the place had gone downhill rapidly in recent years. Many of the units that once housed major retailers now stood empty. Those that were still in use had been occupied by a seedy assortment of discount stores, take-aways and betting shops. The area was plagued by vandalism and drug-related crime and these days the only reason Marta visited was to carry out repair assessments for VisionPlace. Using the bus rather than walking irked her, but at least the transport cop offered some security.

Approaching the entrance to the run-down mall Marta passed a bunch of teenage boys kicking a plastic bottle to and fro and jeering noisily as they mock-punched one another. Taking a deep breath she gave a single nod and passed into the canyon of graffiti-daubed security shutters, her heart beating ferociously, her back burning beneath their hostile stares. Then came the moment she had been dreading.

'Hey, sister, where you from?'

Don't respond, she told herself, just walk on.

'Aw, cute tits, you getting me hot.'

'Bet your pussy tastes real sweet, honey.'

'Look what I got here, see…'

Marta pressed on, slipping her hand inside her satchel and around the StunMaster. Hearing the shuffle of trainers behind her, the youths' whistles and quickfire taunts, her breathing grew rapid, her chest hot and sweaty. When she spotted the pawnbroker's sign up ahead she picked up speed, striding as fast as she could without breaking into a run. Twenty metres. Fifteen. Ten. Five… At last the reinforced orange door was in front of her and she reached out to press the entry phone. Her pursuers gathered across the mall, jeering and howling and kicking the metal shutters.

'Heh, come on, bitch, you ain't tried the goods yet.'

'You gonna get Big E to kick our ass?'

More laughter and shouts and then the door opened and there was Enver, in hoodie and shorts, grinning and ushering her inside as the gang's taunts segued into greetings.

'Hey, E-Man, we like your girlfriend. You wanna share?'

Enver gave the group a friendly wave then, thankfully, shut the door.

'My neighbours like you,' he said cheerfully. 'That's cool.'

*

Enver's apartment above the Red Way retail units was considerably larger than Marta's place, but little time or money appeared to have been invested in its decoration. The walls of the living area and kitchenette were whitewashed and bare, the wood laminate floor uncovered. The furniture was equally sparse, limited to a single two-seater sofa, where Marta sat, and a sturdy, well-worn comfy chair, occupied by Enver. Opposite them was a huge wall-mounted comscreen, between them a square glass-topped coffee table bearing a single gaming handset and an ashtray overflowing with butts. Over by the rear wall stood a bench press, its barbell loaded with some seriously heavy-duty weights.

Enver was a cordial host, over the moon to have Marta visit him, eager to provide her with coffee, which she accepted, and cake, which she declined. Unlike so many men he was willing to listen patiently, too. At first, unused to sharing the details of her private life with anyone bar Dina, Marta found it hard to explain why it was so important they meet that day. But Enver's calm demeanour and gentle encouragement helped her to get through the story and on to the point of her being there, to ask for his help. As the telling progressed, Marta found sharing her sordid tale with someone she barely knew actually provided immense relief. Arpad's claim to be working undercover, which she had intended to keep from Enver, in the end slipped out unchecked. He didn't seem fazed at all.

'That's OK,' he said, much to Marta's relief. 'In my line of business you make a lot of contacts in the police. I can check that out, no problem.'

The question of what Marta actually wanted him to do was not discussed in detail, other than for one point.

'So, let me be clear, Marta,' Enver said, brushing the cake crumbs from his enormous thighs, 'you're not asking me to arrange for the... disappearance of this animal?'

'Oh, good God, no!' Marta said, aghast. 'I just want him to stop.'

Enver sat back on his chair, lit a cigarette and thought for a while.

'OK, no problem, we'll just warn him off.'

Marta gave a nod and smiled awkwardly, aware of having crossed some kind of personal Rubicon.

FIFTEEN

When the caller's ID flashed up on her screen, Marta's first thought was that there must be a problem with the skylight repairs. Pulling on her headphones and smiling her warmest salutation she pressed the accept button.

'Hello, Mr Brancusi. How may I help you?'

He looked rough, even worse than he had done when they had met outside the school. His hair was uncombed and a dark band of stubble covered his chin and pale sunken cheeks. His smile looked weird, too, as though just speaking was an effort.

'Good morning, Ms Ionescu. I'm sorry to call you at work, this was the only number on your card. I'll come straight to the point, I'm not calling about the skylight, I have a favour to ask.'

His admission made her nervous. All calls in and out of the bureaus were recorded and archived. What's more, David might listen in at any time on one of his periodic quality checks. She knew she needed to keep things squeaky clean but this was still a customer, and a high-profile one at that.

'Mr Brancusi,' she said, lowering her voice so as not to attract Dina's attention. 'I'm afraid I can't take personal calls on this line. If you'd like to leave me your contact details...'

His smile vanished and all of a sudden he looked frail and twitchy.

'Oh, sure, I'm sorry.'

Marta turned up the volume on her phone as she jotted down his number. He had a lovely voice, cultivated and gentle despite the nerves. But why was he calling her? And what was the favour he wanted to ask?

Twenty minutes later, on her way back from the restroom, Marta stopped off at an unoccupied touchdown zone and called Michael on her palmcom. The moment he picked up she apologised that she could only spare a few minutes.

'No worry, Ms Ionescu, I'll get straight to the point. It's my daughter, Steffi. As I mentioned when we met, she's having some difficulties at school. She's got mixed up with a bad crowd and I've grounded her for the rest of the holiday. What I'm after is… well, I'd really appreciate your advice. I wondered if we might meet up…'

His voice tailed off and he grimaced.

'Oh, don't worry. In public, everything above board.'

Marta realised that he had misread her expression. She was not afraid of him; rather, she felt for him and his daughter. His was such a familiar story, and one she knew rarely ended well.

'That's not a problem, Mr Brancusi. I finish at four and have to change at Central. Why don't we meet downtown somewhere?'

His frail smile returned.

'Marvellous! Do you know Café Janoui, just around the corner from New City Hall?'

'The place with the potted magnolias outside?'

'That's the one.'

'Sure. I could be there for, say, four-thirty. Does that work for you?'

'Excellent, thank you so much. I'll see you there then.'

They ended the call and Marta headed back to the bureau, the man's thanks ringing in her ears. She felt sorry that he had had to call a stranger for help with his own daughter, but flattered, too, that he had thought of her. She hoped she would be able to help.

*

Marta got to the café a couple of minutes late, breathing hard after practically jogging the half kilometre or so from the terminus. Seeing no sign of Michael she sat down at a vacant pavement table and picked up the menu, glad of the chance to catch her breath before he arrived. She was apprehensive about their meeting but excited, too. His mysterious phonecall had helped to take her mind off things and, anyway, helping others resolve their problems was what she did; it was what she was good at. As a kid in Rietsa her mother was forever chiding her for putting out scraps for stray dogs or bringing back orphaned birds from the fields. Things hadn't changed.

Marta's thoughts were interrupted by the smell of fresh bread drifting out from the café's shadowy interior, reminding her that she needed to pick up something for dinner. Returning to the menu she started to run down the beverages options, just as Michael appeared.

'I'm so sorry I'm late,' he said, as they shook hands. 'I got an urgent call just as I was leaving.'

He looked a lot better than he had that morning, wearing a smart fawn suit and fashionable sunglasses, his hair combed, his face shaved.

'No problem, I've only just arrived myself.'

Michael pulled out the chair opposite Marta and sat down. When he took off his sunglasses she could see the tiredness again in his eyes, but at least his smile suggested that he was a bit more relaxed than when they had spoken that morning.

'Are you hungry, would you like something to eat?'

'I'm tempted but I haven't had my swim today so I'd best stay clear of the cakes and pastries. A coffee'll do fine, thanks.'

'I can recommend the latte.'

'Great.'

After waving to the waiter standing by the café door Michael fixed his eyes on hers.

'I'm so grateful to you for this, Ms Ionescu. I really have been at my wits' end.'

'Please, it's Marta.'

'Then make that Michael,' he said.

The smiling, moustachioed waiter arrived at their table.

'Good afternoon, Mr Brancusi.'

'Dmitri. We'll have two lattes, please.'

The waiter scribbled on his pad and departed.

Marta was impressed with Michael's easy authority.

'So you're a regular here?'

'Yes, I work in New City Hall...'

Michael's smile faltered.

'...Well, I just started back today. I've been off since... Union House.'

Marta gave a consoling smile.

'Of course... So, what do you do at New City Hall?'

'Oh, I work in Transportation. Make sure that the trams and buses run on time, that kind of thing. And what about you, how long have you been with VisionPlace?'

'Six years, ever since they took over the council's property portfolio. Before that I worked in the old Housing Department.'

The man's eyes lit up and Marta could see that, behind all the worry and grief, here was one of life's enthusiasts.

'You know, I hear a lot of people say that things have improved enormously since housing was privatised. I've often wondered if the city wouldn't have been better served handing over the whole UES electrification project to the private sector, too.'

'Well, it worked for me. New premises, better equipment... But, heh, you didn't ask me here to talk about work.'

Michael's smile faded and the haunted look she had seen that morning returned. He leaned forward and lay his forearms on the tablecloth.

'Yes, I... as I said this morning, I could really do with... Well, I'm not sure. You see, Steffi's gone and got mixed up with a fellow student who's in court next week. She's admitted that she's dabbled with drugs and she's started lying to me about her whereabouts...'

The waiter arrived and placed their coffees on the table.

'You have to understand, Ms... Marta... This is a girl who's always delivered straight As, who's never let us down.'

Marta nodded.

'Does your daughter know you're meeting me?'

'No, I've not said anything to her.'

'Good. So d'you know where is she now, I mean, right this minute?'

'Yes, she's back home with our housekeeper.'

'OK, go on.'

'Well, that's about it, really. The Principal thinks this is all a reaction to her mother's passing, but I'm not so sure. Apparently she and this other girl buddied up some time before Sophie died. Maybe she was already building up to some kind of teenage rebellion. Maybe there's something else that none of us know anything about.'

Michael sat back in his chair and let out a sigh before picking up his glass and studying its contents. Marta was moved; she felt desperately sorry for the guy. The only news she had heard about Union House lately concerned rebuilding schedules and engineering allocations. His story provided a very different take on the bomb's impact.

'So, how do you think I can help?'

Michael glanced across at the office workers assembling noisily beneath a nearby beech tree.

'The Principal's taken a hard line. He won't have her back in school after the vacation unless she signs up to their 3D programme. She'll—'

'3D programme?'

'Oh, I'm sorry. Don't Do Drugs. She'll have to undergo daily blood tests, visit the psychologist every week…'

The words were starting to tumble from his lips.

'…But at the moment she seems so fragile, on edge. I blame myself, of course, there's been a lot of stuff come out about how we – her mother and I – how we were always too busy with our careers, that sort of thing, but I—'

Marta raised her hand.

'Michael, heh, slow down, I need to take this in. Look, I'm not a therapist, I just run a weekly youth club.'

'Sure, I know. But, I think she needs something else, someone older and more experienced she can talk to. She's become so angry and defiant.'

'You mean a mother substitute?'

'No, no, not that exactly. Look, our family's small and we're spread all over the Union. Steffi's grown up without all the cousins and aunts a lot of her classmates have. Now Sophie's gone…'

He ground to a halt, as though he had run out of words. Bereft, he lifted his glass to his lips and sipped his coffee. Marta could see his daughter was not the only one with problems.

'Michael, I think we need to back up a few steps.'

*

The apartment was silent, the lights on low. Marta, in her pyjamas and dressing gown, sat on the sofa, stroking the purring Gypsy and gazing into space.

'Hmm. Let's have a look, eh, boy? COMSCREEN ON.'

The comscreen homescreen lit up.

'SEARCH ON MICHAEL BRANCUSI, CARADEA TRANSPORT.'

A column of results flashes up on the screen and Marta ran through the links on offer.

'SCROLL DOWN. STOP …OPEN.'

A screenview of the selected article appeared: 'NEW CHIEF ENGINEER APPOINTED TO CITY TRANSPORT', dated September 16th 2024. Beneath the headline was a photograph of a younger Michael dressed in a business suit and tie. Marta scanned the opening lines describing the lifelong council employee's rise from apprentice to management roles in Purchasing, Strategy & Planning and Sustainability.

'What about that, boy? So much for "Oh, I make sure the trams and buses run on time." SCROLL DOWN… STOP.'

The next article Marta perused was dated November 21st 2028 and headed: 'REGIONAL COMMISSIONER FOR THE EAST VISITS TRANSPORT DEPOT'. In the middle of the article was a more recent photograph of Michael – now Head of Transport – meeting Commissioner Laszlo Dunai. Marta whistled.

'Ha! Looks like Mrs B wasn't the only mover and shaker in the household.'

*

At around the same time that Marta finished reading up on Michael's career and switched off her comscreen, Arpad emerged from his high-fenced lock-up and closed and padlocked the gate. Looking up and down the quiet, neglected street he cursed to himself and took out his palmcom.

'Radics Construction, Odessa Street. I ordered a taxi for eight-thirty and no-one's here. Where is it?'

Arpad listened impatiently as the agent checked the system.

'Cancelled? I didn't cancel...'

Alarmed, he looked around, just as a grey windowless van, its engine sound disconnected, slid to a halt behind him. The side door sprang open and three men dressed in black and wearing balaclavas jumped out and grabbed him. When Arpad resisted he was hit on the back of the head with a cosh, stunning him and causing him to drop his palmcom.

The men bundled Arpad into the van and two climbed in after him. They were swift and efficient; they had done this kind of thing before. Without a word being spoken the third man, a hulk, picked up the palmcom and dropped it through a nearby drainage grate before clambering aboard the van and yanking the door shut as the vehicle sped off in silence.

SIXTEEN

Great Thursday, on her way home from work, Marta stopped off at her mum's. As expected, the two women were engaged in a flurry of activity, her mother dusting and mopping the hall, Aunt Lisha baking colaci – bread for the dead – to take to Mass that evening. Easter was an incredibly busy time for them, what with all of this housework and cooking on top of an endless cycle of services at St Vincent's, so Marta kept out of the way, perching on the arm of the settee in the living room from where she could speak to both women. Twenty minutes later, having finished her coffee and kissed Aunt Lisha's floury cheek, she picked up the carton of eggs on the table and the paperbacks to be returned to Exchangemart and headed down the hall.

'Do you need another bag?' her mother asked, wheezing audibly as she leant on her brush and watched her daughter pack her satchel.

'No thanks, Mama, I've got plenty of room.'

The old woman reached up and patted her shoulder.

'I'm glad you still like doing them,' she said. 'It's hard enough just dyeing the ones for the kids at church, I don't think I could manage the painting now.'

Marta lifted her jacket from the rail and pulled it on then kissed her mother.

'No problem,' she said, stepping on the security wedge and opening the front door. 'See you Sunday then.'

'Yes, see you Sunday, dear.'

As the door closed behind her Marta felt a surge of relief: for once her mother had made no attempt to persuade her to go to Easter Mass. As for her liking doing the eggs, the old lady was right, although these days her willingness to volunteer was prompted by something other than a simple enjoyment of painting. The annual ritual had become a means of marking the Great Thursdays of her childhood, when she, Aurel and Rica would be corralled in a corner of the kitchen and tasked with preparing the family's Easter eggs while their mother got on with cleaning the cottage and preparing the feast. Doing the eggs was no chore; it helped Marta keep the memory of her brothers alive.

Back at home she hung her damp swimming things in the bathroom and fed Gypsy before preparing a salad for herself which she ate standing up in the kitchen, watching the evening news on the comscreen. Afterwards, she listed all the things she was going to do over Easter, like give the place a thorough clean, shortlist the ideas she had received for the annual club outing and sort out her bank account. She was going to have to be extra careful with her money now that Arpad wasn't around to sub her taxis and clothes. On Easter Sunday she would return to her mother's and Aunt Lisha's for lunch. As for Monday, who knows?

Come eight o'clock, unable to find anything of interest in the schedules, she decided to make a start on the eggs.

'What do you fancy, Gypsy?' she asked her purring companion as she searched the radio for some inspirational sounds. When she came across a vaguely familiar rock song with a furious beat and heroic lyrics she turned up the volume, strode across the room and stood the radio on the coffee table. Then, with one great anthem following another, she danced and skipped her way around the tiny apartment, digging out a towel to spread across the table behind the sofa, retrieving her old paint box and brushes from the back of her wardrobe, lowering the eggs gently into a saucepan of boiling water…

When the eggs had cooled she rubbed their shells with vinegar, rinsing and drying each one on a clean dishcloth before lining them up on the table and standing back to inspect her production line. Satisfied that all was in place, she fetched the shabby, heavily stained book of Easter egg designs from her shelf in the bedroom, sat down at the table and began slowly turning the pages.

As happened every year when Marta attempted to engage with the illustrations, her mind was besieged by a host of memories: her brothers arguing over who had produced the best egg, her mother's swift and painful interventions, her father's consoling words. It was at times like these – Easter, Christmas – that she most missed those orderly, predictable aspects of home life, the comfort of family and her brothers' affection, the certainty of what would happen tomorrow and the day after that. At least this Sunday she, her mother and Aunt Lisha would be cracking these eggs in celebration of the Resurrection, just as they had done every year for as long as she had been alive. Comforted by the spark of warmth that thought provided, Marta dipped her brush in the water and applied it to the crimson paint tablet before selecting an egg and making her first stroke.

It was past midnight by the time she stood up to stretch her arms and rotate her shoulders and survey the six eggs lined up along the edge of the table. She was delighted with her work, the vibrant yellows and blues and reds in the flowers, the sharp, steady lines in the zigzags and diamonds. The buzz of her palmcom so late at night came as a shock. Was her mother OK? Could this be another of Arpad's tricks? In three brisk strides she was over by the breakfast bar, her hand on the device. Tapping the screen she read the brief message and let out a squeal of relief: 'Job done. Sleep tight'.

SEVENTEEN

'Christ is Risen!' The words leaped from Mrs Ionescu's cracked lips as she opened the door to her daughter. 'Happy Easter dear.'

'Happy Easter, Mama,' Marta replied, stepping into the hall and embracing her mother warmly. Since her father died this was the only time of the year when the old lady seemed happy and Marta intended to make the most of it.

'Goodness, your jacket's damp, is it raining?'

'Just a shower. It was all over in a couple of minutes.'

'April rains for men, May for beasts. After all this heat we should be grateful.'

Marta, hanging her jacket on the rail, snorted.

'I'll stick with the sun, thanks. I can never get enough.'

'Ha. For a country girl you don't half spout some nonsense!'

'I'm not a...' Marta snapped, cutting herself short when she noticed the wicked smile spreading over her mother's face. 'OK, you got me, Mama!'

Marta lifted a package from her satchel and positioned herself on her mother's left, her arm extended.

'Come on, let's go and find Aunt L.'

The old woman clung to the proffered support and they headed off slowly down the hallway.

*

'Christ is Risen,' beamed Aunt Lisha, throwing her arms around Marta when she entered the kitchen.

'Happy Easter, Auntie. Come and see the eggs.'

Back in the living room Mrs Ionescu was lowering herself slowly into her chair, her rheumy eyes glued to the parcel her daughter had left on the table. Aunt Lisha sat down beside her sister-in-law, keeping her hands to herself. The annual unwrapping of the eggs was a reminder of their rural traditions, of a time when Ele would jealously guard her role as conductor-in-chief of the family's Easter celebrations. Marta took the third chair, across the table from her mother, praying the old lady would be pleased with her work. Once settled Mrs Ionescu set about undoing the yellow bow that Marta had tied loosely around the egg carton, before moving on to the layers of birthday paper, the only decent wrapping she had been able to find at home. Marta noticed that her mother's hands were shaking more than usual and wondered if this was a symptom of her excitement or yet another sign of her ongoing deterioration.

'Looks like you could do with a glass of palinca, Ele,' Aunt Lisha said, noticing the direction of her niece's gaze.

Mrs Ionescu pursed her lips, focussing all her attention on the task. When she was finished and the plain papier-mâché carton stood uncovered before them she brushed the paper and ribbon aside with a flourish.

'Ready?' she asked, baring her brown, irregular teeth in an eager grin.

Aunt Lisha clapped her hands.

'Come on, Ele, don't keep us waiting.'

Mrs Ionescu lifted the lid and the two women gasped in unison.

'Oh, Marta,' Mrs Ionescu said. 'They're beautiful.' Then she picked up the carton and weighed it in her hands. 'Why on earth didn't you blow them like I told you? They're too perfect to crack.'

'Next year I will,' Marta said. 'I promise.'

'All you need is a little beeswax to seal the holes.'

'Yes, Mama, I know.'

Aunt Lisha picked up one of the eggs and removed her glasses.

'Wonderful work, my dear,' she said, peering at the oak leaf pattern. 'It *would* be nice to have one for our cabinet.'

Popping the egg back in the carton, she stood up, crossed to the dresser and took the white tablecloth from the drawer.

'Just hold the eggs up, Ele, will you, so Marta and I can get this... a bit more your side, Marta... There we are. Perfect.'

After handing out some side plates, she sat back down.

'It's you and me then, Lisha,' said Mrs Ionescu, ready with an egg in her hand and a determined look on her face.

Her opponent selected the oak leaf egg and held it up to signify that she was ready.

'Christ is Risen!' Mrs Ionescu shouted, thrusting the pointed end of her egg forwards.

Marta heard the soft crunch as the two eggs collided, saw the fragments of shell on the tablecloth.

'He is risen indeed!' Aunt Lisha replied, inspecting the damage that her sister-in-law's vigorous assault had inflicted.

Marta could tell from the colour of the eggshell fragments that her aunt had lost the first round. Reaching over to the carton she selected the egg covered with diamonds. She had enjoyed doing this one, finding the straight lines a welcome respite from the demands of all that curly flora.

'Christ is Risen!' came her mother's war-cry, as the two eggs collided.

'He is risen indeed!' Aunt Lisha said when her niece remained silent.

Marta smiled. This time it was her mother's egg that had cracked.

*

Every year Marta was amazed by the quantity of food the two women produced for their Easter celebration and this year was no exception: jellied chicken, rice and pork wrapped in grape leaves, beetroot and potato salads, and a braided loaf topped with feta. It was incredible and, as ever, delicious. After a leisurely and surprisingly harmonious lunch the three women tidied the kitchen and washed up before retiring to the living room. There Aunt Lisha recited verses of poetry she remembered from school whilst Mrs Ionescu read, creakily but with gusto, extracts from St John: 'Woman, behold thy son!' For her contribution, Marta had downloaded an article onto her tablet, a description of the secret Easter celebrations that took place in the city during the Turkish occupation of the seventeenth century. She found the account fascinating but suspected that her relatives' inflated praise was driven more by good manners than a genuine enthusiasm for the subject matter.

Later, whilst her mother and aunt got ready for Vespers, Marta checked the security settings and files on their comscreen. A particularly vicious virus had been doing the rounds, she lied, and she wanted to make sure that it had not penetrated their service provider's firewalls. A quick search of their inbox and archives soon revealed the absence of any mysterious messages or potentially risky links that might have come from Arpad. As a final insurance, Marta picked up the phone that had been sitting untouched on the dresser for weeks and called out.

'If you're not going to use this disposable, I'll take it with me. They're always handy in emergencies.'

'That's fine, dear,' her mother called from the bathroom. 'I told you we didn't need one.'

Marta pocketed the device, hugely relieved that her search had drawn a blank.

'What a popular girl you are! Use the link to see just how popular.'

Arpad's longing for revenge threatened Marta's job, her standing in the community and her legal status as someone deemed fit to work with young people. Hopefully by now, with Enver's encouragement, the cockroach will have removed his filthy fabrication from the grid. There was no way she was going to allow him to win this battle, no way at all.

EIGHTEEN

With the ramping up of the programme to rebuild Union House, more and more inspection requests were being passed to the bureaus. By the end of April Marta was carrying out two or three assessments every week, a big increase on her typical allocation. Normally she would have welcomed the opportunity to be out and about but the Arpad affair had taken its toll and, out on the streets, she felt exposed and vulnerable. Fortunately, she still had Dina to help keep her spirits up. Even though her friend was away on holiday in Marrakech, Marta received messages every day, always upbeat, invariably saucy. The first, received just thirty-six hours after Dina's departure, was typical. Marta was sitting on a tram at the time, on her way to a job:

'Eat your heart out, bitch!'

Scrolling down the page she had chuckled when she saw the photo of Dina, wearing the briefest of bikinis, cuddling up to a gorgeous young hunk in swimming shorts.

'Good on you, girl!' she whispered.

'Heh,' the whiskery pensioner sitting beside her said, leering at the photo. 'Do you think I can be his friend, too?'

The intention had been for Marta to meet Michael and his daughter at some point over the Easter break. However, for various reasons – her shifts, Michael's return to work, Steffi's reluctance to play ball – that had not happened. Throughout, Steffi maintained her refusal to sign the Principal's contract and remained incarcerated at home when the city's schools reopened, with just the family's housekeeper for company. Then, on the evening of the first day of the summer term, Marta received a call from a very animated Michael.

'She's agreed to meet you, no conditions,' he gushed. 'It's a breakthrough, Marta, real progress.'

Marta was delighted that, at last, something had gone Michael's way. She knew well enough from his texts that he and Steffi had been at loggerheads over Easter. Despite that, she did not share his jubilation. Why had the girl capitulated now, she couldn't help wondering, what had changed? That said, Marta still looked forward to meeting the teenager. Prevention, she had long ago learned, was so much easier than cure and if there was anything she could do to help stop this young woman coming off the rails, she wanted to do it. Her motives were not entirely selfless, however. The chance to experience a totally different world, one that offered a bit of glamour and colour beyond the grey, bleak streets of Goval, was hugely attractive and Marta knew she would be lying if she pretended otherwise. And so, on the Tuesday, the last day in April, Marta caught an early bus into Caradea and walked along to Badeni Park, the small, leafy oasis where she was to meet Michael and Steffi. As she entered the park and headed for the outdoor café, the pungent scent of damp vegetation filled her nostrils, reminding her of autumn mornings on the farm. She could almost hear the tractor, the cries of the gulls following in its wake.

The café was deserted so she chose a table on the inner hub, midway between the kiosk and the surrounding path, and sat down. The waiter who served her was a chirpy soul who looked too young to be at work. Seeing his badly crumpled shirt and gnawed nails, she wanted to cook him a good meal. After a brief exchange he returned to the shelter of the kiosk while she snuggled down inside her anorak to sip her cappuccino and watch the budgerigars in the concrete aviary opposite, chattering and whistling and rattling their beaks against the wire. For the first time in days she felt able to relax. She had heard no more from Arpad and 'her' site had been taken down. All searches for her name or linked material on the grid yielded only legitimate references.

Marta caught sight of the Brancusis while they were still some way off: Michael, tall and spindly, his sports jacket and chinos flapping around his long bones; his daughter in a figure-hugging leather jacket and tight jeans, statuesque and moody. They walked apart, aloof from each other and the world around them. Marta imagined the conversation leading up to this moment, the tactics Michael had used to win his daughter round. How had he described her to Steffi? What were the two of them feeling right now?

'Hi,' Michael called out as he made his way between the tables, his exaggerated smile making him look a little crazy. His handshake was firm, though, and full of hope.

'Marta, this is Steffi,' he said, stepping aside. 'Steffi, Marta.'

The girl stayed put and raised her palm American-Indian style.

'How,' she said. 'Woman on roof sent by wicked capitalist landlord.'

Her cultivated voice exuded a manufactured weariness that sent a twinge of inadequacy shooting through Marta's body. She forced a laugh and mimicked the girl's wave.

'Yes, that's us. Exploitation Anonymous.'

Despite wearing flat shoes the kid was a good head taller than her. Her clothes were classy and fitted her perfectly. What must she be thinking, Marta wondered, seeing this short-arse standing in front of her in faded jeans and a worn anorak?

'Fantastic recall, Steffi,' Michael enthused. 'She never forgets a face... Can I get you a top-up, Marta? Cappuccino?'

Marta nodded and the three of them sat down. Seconds later the young waiter arrived and Michael ordered two cappuccinos and a cola.

'Well, this is cosy,' he said with toe-curling jollity. 'So, where shall we start?'

Too quick, Marta thought. Much too quick. But she had come prepared.

'Did you watch the match last night?'

Father and daughter looked at one another and grinned.

'You bet,' Steffi said. 'League champions! I knew they could do it.'

Marta unzipped her anorak. The sun was breaking through the haze and the temperature was starting to rise.

'Yeah, pretty dramatic. I'm not a huge football fan but one of the guys at my club is trialling for Dynamo so I have to stay up to speed.'

'Really?' said Michael. 'Who's that?'

'Paolo Gheorghiu.'

'Wow, really?' Michael said. 'We know him alright, we watch all the youth games.'

Steffi started weaving her hands about, recreating the chip and swerve Paolo had executed in his latest game before scoring.

'That last goal of his was ace,' she said. 'I don't know why Dynamo haven't signed him already.'

Marta was warming to the girl. Once she let her guard down she wasn't so bad after all.

'It won't be long, I'm sure,' she said. 'He's full of confidence and knows what he wants.'

The girl laughed.

'He's a looker, too. Maybe you can get me a date?'

Michael spluttered in his coffee and rapped the table with his knuckles.

'Order, ladies, please. Can I just say, I think it's great that Dynamo are through to the semi-finals for the first time but maybe that's enough football for now, eh?'

The three of them laughed and Marta felt herself relax. They had got off to a good start. But then Michael started telling her all about his meeting the previous day at the Diocesan office, discussing arrangements for his wife's memorial service, and she felt the focus of their conversation starting to drift. Why had he brought this up now? As she listened to him rattling on she got the feeling that he was fond of hearing his own voice. There again, perhaps she was being unkind; maybe he was simply trying to help his daughter settle in. Or maybe he was the one who was nervous? Whatever, his talkativeness did at least provide Marta with the opportunity to observe how the two of them interacted. The results were certainly illuminating.

'We don't believe in hiding Sophie away, do we, love?' he said at one point, eliciting a resigned shake of the head from his daughter. 'She brought happiness into our lives,' he declared later on. 'We're determined to celebrate that fact, aren't we, Steff?'

To Marta, Michael came across as someone who had extremely high expectations of his daughter and who liked everything just so. And, while Steffi appeared sharp and witty, she seemed quite in awe of her father at times. It was, thought Marta, a familiar ambivalence, that fraught eruption in family life when teenagers started to kick against their parents' authority and world-view. Only, of course, in this case the death of Steffi's mother had clearly complicated—

'I'm just popping over to the office,' Michael announced, getting to his feet and straightening his jacket. 'There's something I need to do. I won't be long.'

The look of shock on Steffi's face told Marta that this move had not been planned. It was a cheap trick to play, pretending they were here for a three-way meeting then disappearing.

'Fancy another drink?' Marta said when Michael had left.

The girl shook her head.

'No... Thanks.'

Marta decided against a third coffee. If she had to go for a pee before Michael got back the kid would probably disappear.

'Look, I know this must be tough for you, Steffi, but your dad's just trying to do what he thinks is best. It's not easy for him either.'

Steffi stared at her like she was a piece of dirt.

'You won't take my mother's place,' she said calmly, her pale green eyes unblinking. 'I'll make sure of that.'

The bitch is trying to needle me, Marta thought, her patience fading fast. But she needed to stay calm, at least until Michael returned.

'Let's get something clear, shall we? Your dad approached *me* and asked *me* for help. I'm not trying to replace your mum or be your best buddy or steal your inheritance. In fact...'

So much for staying calm.

'...In fact,' she continued, lowering her voice, 'I know how you're hurting right now. My two brothers were killed in a road accident nearly twenty years ago and I still think about them most days. No-one – no boyfriend or girlfriend, neighbour or teacher, not even my mum or dad – ever came near to taking their place in here.'

She tapped her chest.

'But that doesn't mean I've shut myself off. You hold the things, the people, that are dear to you in your heart and you move on. I know, right now, you probably can't imagine how that will happen but I can tell you it will, just give it time.'

Steffi looked away and Marta followed her gaze, over to the kiosk where a young woman with an empty pushchair was talking to the waiter. The couple's laughter, the proximity of their bodies, the way the woman touched the boy's shirt sleeve suggested that they knew each other well. Whatever their relationship, the woman's daughter – a toddler with an amazing head of ginger curls – seemed uninterested. She was far too busy chattering away into the banana the waiter had given her.

'Mrs Carp? I'd like a kilo of sugar and three oranges, please. Oh, and…'

When Steffi turned back Marta noticed her eyes were glistening.

'What a great life,' the teenager said, taking out her handkerchief. 'Oh, to be a kid again.'

Marta's heart went out to this troubled young woman. What on earth could she do to help her?

NINETEEN

During the week following Marta's meeting with the Brancusis the heatwave that had gripped southern Europe grew in ferocity. In Caradea the afternoon temperature hovered around thirty-seven degrees for days on end and the air hardly moved. Dirty yellow clouds hung over East and West Parks. In the city's parched gardens flowers wilted and grass died; in exposed streets the tarmac melted. St Paul's-on-the-Hill shimmered for hours in the unhindered sunlight and the river fell to its lowest level in years. Power outages were widespread. Tempers flared and assaults rose steeply but the police were not the only public servants who were overstretched: the fire service was called out repeatedly to break into fortified apartments where the elderly occupants had expired. In Goval and the city's other grim estates, babies died in their cots in stifling bedrooms while their parents got stoned or turned tricks. All people could do was struggle on with their lives and pray for rain.

*

Michael paused and mopped his forehead with his handkerchief.

'I tell you, the apartment's been like a war zone this weekend,' he said, waving for service. 'Thank God she's gone back to school.'

Marta could understood now why Michael had sounded so frazzled when he had called last night, why he had been so keen to meet up before work. Things had clearly gone downhill fast. The temperature wasn't helping either. Despite the huge umbrellas erected over the tables outside Café Janoui, both of them were suffering, Michael sweating profusely, Marta uncomfortably aware of the moisture trickling down her spine. She was grateful for every tram and delivery vehicle that passed their table. Without them, there would have been no breeze at all.

'It's the heat,' she said, glancing at the women on the next table, fanning themselves. 'It's driving everyone nuts.'

'Whatever it is, I can't take much more. If the two of us carry on like this we're going to come to blows, I know it.'

'Mr Brancusi?'

Marta recognised the smiley waiter who had served them the last time they were here.

'Could I have another lemonade, Dmitri. Marta?'

'Er, I'll have an iced tea.'

The waiter picked up their glasses and headed back inside. Marta leaned forwards and lowered her voice.

'So, d'you think she wants to abandon the programme?'

Michael groaned.

'That's my worry. But if she drops out she'll have to leave Natalia High. And what school will accept her once they know what's been going on?'

Marta looked at his skewed tie and bloodshot eyes and felt desperately sorry for the man. Last week in Badeni Park he had seemed so full of hope.

'It's such a shame,' she said, shaking her head. 'You fight for two days and end up where you started.'

'Tell me about it!'

Their drinks arrived and Michael guzzled his down feverishly, allowing Marta time to think about what she had heard. At the moment she just couldn't see how she could help him, especially given how poorly her first meeting with Steffi had gone.

'If we'd hit it off, Michael, I'd be happy to meet up again. But going by what you've told me, there's no way she's going to want to listen to me. Perhaps when things settle down, when she's used to being on the 3D pro—'

Michael waved his hands.

'No, no, no! Surely it must be worth trying? Maybe if she was on home territory, if you were to come over for dinner, say?'

His voice tailed off, leaving his eyes to do the pleading. Even as she replied, Marta got the feeling she was making a big mistake.

'All right, I'll come round. But give it a few days; she needs time to get used to the situation. She's lost her mum and her crush has gone to jail. Now practically her every move is monitored. The kid needs a break!'

Michael's face lit up and he seized her hand.

'Thank you, Marta, thank you so much. That means the world to me.'

'I said I'd try, there's no guarantees.'

Michael withdrew his hand and sat back.

'I meant to ask about the power cuts in Goval. How have you been coping?'

Marta snorted.

'Well, it's hardly the weather to be without aircon, is it? I just try and keep still and drink plenty. I told my mum and aunt to run a cold bath and lie in it for a while.'

'And did they?'

'Nah, I think they prayed instead.'

Michael smiled and checked the time on his palmcom.

'I'm sorry,' he said, lifting his jacket from the back of the chair. 'I have to go, I'm meeting my boss at eleven. Are you going to stay here for a while?'

'No, I can always flex on early, build up my holiday bank. At least it's cool at work.'

They finished their drinks and stood up.

'I'll get these,' he said, holding out his hand. 'And thanks again for meeting me like this. You're a lifesaver.'

They shook hands.

'Let me know how Steffi's doing and we'll fix a date, OK?'

Michael nodded and gave her a brave smile before heading over to Dmitri to settle up. Out on the street, Marta turned and watched him stride up the hill. She wished she could have given the poor devil a hug.

*

Marta was delighted to see the look on Gyula Bokros's face when she emerged from the security vestibule at Roman House. After her last meeting with Steffi she had regretted not taking greater care over her appearance. Tonight, she had worn her black and silver dress and draped her silk shawl across her shoulders to show Michael and Steffi that she, too, could put on a show when she wanted. But wearing the Dagol was not just about impressing the Brancusis. In the continuing heatwave the absence of a back and sleeves provided some much-needed ventilation. The concierge's bulging eyes were a bonus; she had not anticipated such a spontaneous response from the man who, last time they met, had been so stuffy.

'Good evening, Ms Ionescu,' he said as she crossed the reception area. 'I've informed Mr Brancusi that you're here, please go on up.'

As she stepped into the antique lift and closed the grille, Marta felt her heart beating against her ribs. Steffi had calmed down, apparently, and she and her father had not argued for several days. But Marta was determined to remain on her guard. Helping this damaged couple was not going to be easy. But then, what had been lately?

Michael was waiting for her outside the apartment, looking very relaxed in his casual clothes – blue-striped shirt, stone chinos, loafers. Unfortunately, the weight he was stacking on was, Marta knew, due to comfort eating rather than any improvement in his emotional state. Over the past fortnight they had lunched together three times at Café Janoui and in that time she had seen him go from a bowl of soup to a two-course meal with mountains of pasta and bread.

'Wow, Marta, you look like a movie star!'

'Heh, you ain't kiddin' me any, I met your kind before.'

Michael frowned.

'Sorry. Mae West. I have a… friend who likes old movies.'

'Oh. Right.'

His kiss was tentative but she did not mind. It was nice just not being taken for granted. 'Can I take your shawl?' he asked after closing the door.

She handed him the shawl and he hung it carefully on the coat rack before turning to her and smiling.

'Right, let's get a drink, shall we? Steff's out on the balcony.'

As they walked down the hall, Marta realised that she felt much more at ease in the apartment this time round. The décor was still too staid for her liking, the silence just as strange, but the evening sunlight had cast a golden glow over the space beneath the skylight that made it feel much more welcoming than she remembered. When they arrived at the door at the end of the hall and Michael reached for the handle, she touched his arm lightly.

'How's she been today?' she whispered.

'OK,' he said, without hesitation. 'She did her homework this morning, practised her violin, called her friends. Maybe she's tired of fighting, Marta. I know I am.'

'Let's hope you're right.'

Michael opened the door and Marta entered to experience her second surprise of the evening. Having been up on the roof she knew the apartment's rough dimensions but she had not given much thought as to how the space below might be divided up. The room was enormous, at least ten metres square, with four sofas over by the top-of-the-range comscreen and a long mahogany dining table at the opposite end. It was also much brighter than the hall, with pale walls, few pictures and windows on two sides, plus a gorgeous open-plan kitchen off to the right with loads of wood cupboards and shiny appliances. It was like something from the glossy magazines at the hairdressers, Marta thought, turning around to find Michael standing behind her, a melancholy expression on his face.

'I'm sorry, wandering round like I own the place. It's amazing.'

'We fell for it on our first visit,' he said. 'It's been our only home since we married.'

Marta hesitated. She knew how fretful Michael had been lately and wanted to avoid upsetting him.

'Well, I think you and Sophie have done a great job... And something's smelling pretty good, too.'

'Oh, I can't claim credit for that. Maria, our housekeeper, is a wonderful cook. She makes a batch of stews and soups every week and leaves them for us in the freezer. We're spoilt rotten. Anyhow, what can I get you to drink?'

'I'll have a red wine, please.'

'Excellent. Steffi's out there,' he said, waving at the French windows in the far corner of the room. 'Why don't you go and join her and I'll bring our drinks out?'

'OK,' Marta replied, starting across the room towards the open windows.

Stepping out onto the balcony Marta was wowed by the sights and sounds that greeted her, the jumble of old and modern buildings opposite, the bustle of people and traffic at the junction down below. Steffi, dressed in branded jeans and a loose silk blouse, her hair up and braided in the German style, was sitting at a small circular table to Marta's left, tapping on her palmcom.

'Hi,' Marta said, suddenly feeling over-dressed.

Steffi looked up and smiled stiffly.

'Hi,' she said before continuing her tapping.

Marta crossed to the balustrade and gazed out over the Old City.

'That's one hell of a view.'

She turned and faced the young woman.

'Your hair looks great.'

Steffi put her palmcom down on the table.

'My mum used to do it like this for me when I was a kid. I thought I'd give it a go.'

Marta pulled out a chair and sat down opposite the teenager.

'Well, it's certainly worked, you look fantastic... So, how are things?'

Steffi sighed and fidgeted with her palmcom.

'Shitty. The teachers are oozing understanding, the psychologist's a fucking dork... And I miss Petra. She didn't deserve three years, not for a few lousy tabs and a slap.'

Marta, seduced by the setting sun's glow, the slight breeze brushing her face, pondered what to say next.

'I love your dress,' Steffi continued. 'Where did you get it?'

'It was a present. From Kiev.'

'From a boyfriend?'

Marta laughed. There's no flies on this kid!

'Yes, but we're not together now.'

'Oh. I'm sorry.'

'I'm not,' Marta said, draping her arm over the stonework before immediately jerking it back. 'Wow! That's hot!'

Steffi giggled.

'Be careful, in this temperature the stone can burn.'

Their eyes met and Steffi smiled, just as the French windows opened and Michael stepped out and placed a glass of red wine on the table next to Marta.

'I'm sorry for the delay, I was just… What's so funny then?'

'Marta put her arm on the balustrade, Dad.'

'Ah yes, you need to watch out, Marta, the stone can get very hot.'

Steffi grinned at Marta, a knowing, naughty smirk.

'OK, OK,' Michael said, holding up his hands. 'Do you want a top-up, love?'

'Yes, please,' Steffi replied, handing her father her empty glass.

On returning with his own and Steffi's drinks Michael started to tell Marta about the jumble of architecture visible from the balcony, the various Ottoman and Hapsburg landmarks spread across the valley. Marta could happily have listened to his polished voice for hours but she was aware that Steffi had picked up her palmcom again and was playing no part in the conversation. Fortunately, as the sun's pink rays lit up their faces and the air filled with the sound of birds preparing to roost, Michael's wristwatch started beeping.

'Ah, dinner's ready,' he said, downing the remainder of his wine. 'Let's eat.'

Inside, after instructing his daughter to make sure that their guest was comfortable, Michael marched through to the kitchen area, pulled on a chequered apron and busied himself with the starter. Marta surveyed the sparkling crystal and gleaming silverware set out neatly around the near end of the dining table and wondered if the Brancusis ever sat in front of the comscreen and shared a pizza.

'You sit here, Marta,' Steffi said, tapping the chair closest to them. 'I'll sit opposite and Dad can go at the head. He likes to be in charge.'

Marta sat down, amused by the girl's wink and curious about her motives in placing her opposite the colour portrait of her glamorous mother.

'My great-grandmother use to have a tablecloth like this in her trousseau,' Marta said, running her fingertips over the ornate damask cloth. 'I think my mum's still got it somewhere.'

Steffi put down her glass and raised her clear green eyes. A superior smile spread across her lips.

'I haven't seen this one for ages. You're highly honoured.'

Marta sipped her wine. She'd thought, out there on the balcony, that she was getting somewhere.

'Grub up,' Michael barked, striding across the carpet in his apron, an ornate tureen grasped firmly between two enormous oven gloves.

The first course was hard going, conversation flaring up and dying away like sunshine on a cloudy day. Steffi remained resolutely quiet, responding to the adults' enquiries with stock replies and evasive glances, whilst Michael's earnest account of the Platinum League semi-final, which Dynamo had lost two-nil, depressed them all. Marta was surprised and disappointed to discover that neither Steffi nor her father read any fiction for pleasure. Meanwhile, listening to the slurp of soup and chink of spoons, she began to wonder why they were avoiding talking about the 3D programme, why Michael had bothered to invite her here at all.

Thankfully, things picked up during the main course – a delicious beef stew – when Michael asked Marta about growing up in the country, a subject they had not discussed previously. It felt a bit like being interviewed for a job but it did at least give Marta the chance to try and cheer them up a bit; as things stood they were all in danger of dying of boredom. Ignoring the negatives, her memories of hard labour and poisonous village politics, she delivered an idyllic account of life in Rietsa, harvesting potatoes, milking cows, helping her mother make jams and pickles. With each line she could feel the Brancusis drawing closer, could see from the growing gleam in their eyes that they were starting to relax. Both of them laughed when Marta told them the story about the horse taking off without her, spilling the day's pickings from the wagon as it raced through the village.

'So, why did you leave the farm?' Michael asked later, refilling Marta's wineglass.

'We had to sell up; the bigger operations were undercutting us on everything. My dad tried selling a field here and there at first but by the late nineties the writing was on the wall. His family had farmed that land for five generations, but they just couldn't survive the changes that came after 1989.'

Steffi frowned: 'The revolution?'

'That's right, love,' her father purred.

'Yeah,' Marta continued, 'my dad didn't stop going on about it until the day he died. "We managed to hang on for forty years under the communists," he used to say, "but capitalism did for us in ten."'

Steffi's eyes met hers and Marta got the feeling that at last she was making progress, that here was a chance to start building something, so long as Michael didn't interfere.

'So, why *didn't* you stay in the country?' the girl asked. 'I mean, why did you move here?'

'It turned out my dad had borrowed a lot of money to keep the farm going and buy off the local officials. There was hardly anything left when we finally sold it. Anyhow, things were changing fast; farming wasn't about people anymore. The big agrochemical companies brought in their seed cartels and genetic patents, the small farm holdings failed one by one. The village just withered away.'

'Was that why your brothers had to leave?' Steffi asked.

Marta froze, uncomfortable that the one subject she had scrupulously avoided mentioning had been raised.

'You have brothers?' Michael asked, surprised.

'No, Dad,' Steffi cried, seeing the look on Marta's face. 'She...'

But it was too late, something inside Marta had already snapped. The years of grieving, the stress of the last few weeks, the evening's tensions... It was all too much. A wave of sadness swept through her body, an overwhelming regret. Why had she wasted her life for so long? Why had she missed the chance to produce something like the beautiful, thoughtless creature sitting opposite her? She opened her mouth to speak but nothing came out. She looked at Steffi, then at Michael and still nothing came, until, all of a sudden, as if to compensate for her tongue's silence, the tears spilled from her eyes.

'I did have, two of them,' she cried, wiping her face with her napkin. 'They were killed in a road smash in France... They'd gone there looking for work.'

'Oh, Marta,' Michael said, the regret clear in his eyes. 'I'm so sorry.'

Steffi jumped up and came around and threw her arms around the older woman, holding her head tight against her chest. The feel of that young embrace, the sound of her voice – 'It's OK, Marta, I've got you' – brought a sweet, mournful relief. *So this is what it feels like...* And then she laughed and the tears came afresh and Steffi started crying, too, the two of them sniffing and wailing as Michael swayed uncomfortably in his seat, looking bemused and not quite sure what to do. And then he, too, got to his feet and wrapped his long arms around the two of them and stood there, silent and impassive but undeniably present.

*

Marta was shocked by what happened at the Brancusis' place. She rarely shed tears, alone or in company, but for it to happen on such an important occasion, when somebody else was meant to be the focus of the evening, was mortifying. She had not realised just how wound up the Arpad business had got her, how much she still grieved for Aurel and Rica. That said, sitting in that huge room, drinking the brandy that Michael urged on her and talking about her beautiful boys, she experienced an immense relief. At one point, she felt as though she might explode with love. And all the while these two people, strangers a few weeks ago and suffering their own much fresher tragedy, had listened patiently to her prattling and smiled and asked questions and embraced her again when the tears threatened to return. When she had finished, her tale done, she had felt energised and ready to carry on, to do the job that had brought her to Roman House in the first place. Steffi's timely invitation to her room, supposedly to listen to music, had signalled that their relationship was changing fast, that she, too, wanted a break from her father's towering presence. She was ready to talk.

In many ways the girl was a mirror image of her father. She spoke in that same analytical, detached manner as him and possessed, once she dropped her guard and stopped playing games, the same gentle wit. But the world she described to Marta that evening, the weird, parallel world she had taken to visiting prior to her discovery, was not one her father would have appreciated hearing about, with its drugs and casual sex, its cynicism, even hatred. To see her sprawled over that bed with its ivory duvet and lace trimmings, bemoaning the country's loss of national identity and the influx of illegals, gave Marta the creeps. The more she heard, though, the more she got the impression that Steffi was relaying someone else's views, a friend or lover, maybe, or an activist like the strident young men and women she, Marta, used to march with. It all sounded so rehearsed, and yet curiously flat, too, as though she was doing her damnedest to appear detached from it all.

'Nah, taking drugs isn't so cool,' she said at one point, 'and I don't know what all the fuss is about sex... Being with Petra was what mattered, the tabs and the rest of it were neither here nor there.'

Michael had been right: Steffi's attachment, the changes in her behaviour, were already well underway months before her mother had died. That said, as she listened to the increasingly random outpourings of this disturbed young woman, the timing of events turned out to be one of the few issues Marta could grasp with any certainty. That and Steffi's bitter resentment at being an only child, her being deprived of the company of brothers and sisters. Elsewhere, her ambiguous and contradictory statements made it impossible to pin down her true thoughts and feelings. She claimed to miss her mother but did not appear to be grieving in any conventional sense. She insisted that she loved and respected her father, and yet her description of his drinking and his obsession with keeping her mother's memory alive bordered on the scornful. Through all of this, one fact stood out: over the years Steffi had built a wall around herself to keep her parents at arms' length.

'Yes,' she said, confirming Marta's observation. 'Ours is a household of achievers; we don't do emotion very well.'

At this point Steffi had paused her music player – the furious, thrashing songs that acted as cover, Marta suspected, in case Michael was loitering in the hall – and gone off to the bathroom. When she returned Marta had taken the opportunity to ask again about the 3D programme.

'I told you,' Steffi snapped. 'I'm going through the motions, staying clean. I hate it, it's so demeaning being tested every day.'

'So, definitely no further... experimentation... since Petra's departure?'

'No.'

Steffi pulled a face and punched her pillow and Marta worried that she might have blown it. But then the girl slipped to the floor and pulled a small black cabin suitcase from beneath the bed. Taking a key from the pocket of her jeans she unlocked and opened the case and took out a shoe box which, after removing the lid, she placed carefully on the bed next to Marta.

'Look,' she said, still kneeling on the carpet. 'I want to show you something.'

Marta looked down at the photo-booth shots of Steffi with a spikey-haired goth – studs in her nose and eyebrows and lips – pulling faces at the camera, a bundle of handwritten notes bound with a scarlet ribbon, a lock of black hair in a little plastic bag, a single razor blade...

'Go ahead, Marta, have a read, it's Petra's poetry. Christ, she'd kill me if she knew I was showing you all this.'

*

It was gone midnight when Marta finally left after promising Steffi she would call. Michael came down in the lift with her, chatting away as though he had hosted a happy, carefree meal rather than back-to-back therapy sessions with two emotionally labile females. Outside, standing in the warm night air, he thanked her profusely and insisted on paying for the taxi.

'It's the least I can do,' he said, swiping his palmcom across the auto-toll, 'given everything you've done for us.'

When she'd taken her seat in the rear of the taxi he leaned in and told her he was so sorry about her brothers, then kissed her on the cheek and closed the door. They waved to one another as the taxi pulled off from the kerb, once more when it turned into Zal. Then Marta sat back in her seat and closed her eyes, grateful that the driver was not a talker. She felt exhausted, drained by her own disclosures and by the demands of listening to a young woman's tales of near self-destruction. *Christ, the girl is a mess!* So much energy and emotion wasted looking for a little love, the same old tale she had heard so often from so many kids. And here she was with so much love of her own to give and instead all she does is spend her days in a half-dark room talking about blocked drains and broken lifts, rental rates and man hours per job. Well, she might not be able to do something for all the unhappy kids in this poor, broken-down world but she could help one for sure.

And there and then Marta decided that she would drop the idea of putting in for a transfer or finding a new job away from Caradea. Given everything that had happened tonight there was no way she could just up and abandon the Brancusis. She had responsibilities now, commitments to them both. And they needed her.

TWENTY

Marta and Dina sat in the shade of the canopy, sipping their long, cool mixers and trying to keep as still as possible. This was the first time the two women had spent time together since Dina's return from holiday, alternate shifts and days off having conspired to keep them apart. It had been Marta's suggestion that they stop off in town on their way home from work but, within minutes of sitting down, she had started to regret opening her mouth. There were just two other couples sitting at Grul's outside tables and, with the square bereft of the usual throng of pedestrians, its beautiful fountain switched off, the place was eerily quiet. Worse, Marta soon found herself becoming intensely irritated by Dina's self-obsessed chatter, bored with the accounts of her sexual antics. Marta's relationship with Michael and Steffi had exploded into her life and, right now, she found them much more interesting.

'Yeah, we spent two days in bed,' Dina said, resuming her account of the holiday's highs and lows. 'It was glorious... Then the next day he takes off with some teenager with big tits from the hotel next door. Bastard!'

'Well, at least you got a good tan,' Marta said, trying to display some enthusiasm, if only for Dina's deep chestnut glaze.

'Yeah, I guess... Talking of men, what's "Psycho" been up to?'

Dina's question sent a shiver down Marta's spine. She was trying hard to put the Arpad days behind her but it was proving impossible. Barely a day passed when she didn't wonder what Enver had done to get that vile website taken down. Meanwhile, on the two Fridays that Enver had worked at the club since their meeting at his place, they had hardly spoken. It was as though both wanted to avoid being tainted by any association with Arpad and his sordid world.

'It's all gone quiet. I... I think he got the message there's no way we're getting back together again.'

Dina scowled.

'So what's eating you then? I might as well have been talking to the fucking wall as sitting here with you tonight!'

Marta was taken aback; she thought she had been quite chatty, considering.

'What do you mean? We've talked plenty.'

'Sure we've talked, but you've not been present. It's that faraway look, Marta; you're either worrying about something or you've got a new man. Or both! Don't try and bluff me, I—'

A squad car shot across the square, its lights flashing and siren wailing, drowning out Dina's voice and forcing a brief interlude in their exchange. After the vehicle had disappeared down a narrow side street a peeved Marta delivered her response.

'That's nonsense. Why the hell would I be looking for another bloke when I've only just got rid of one?'

'You tell me. Something's bothering you!'

Marta looked at the concerned expression on Dina's face, the unflinching stare. She was a good friend, and Marta owed her.

'Do you want a another drink?'

Dina put on her sulky face.

'Only if you make it worth my while.'

Marta waved to the waiter standing by the café door.

'Well, I don't know about that, but I can tell you what's been happening while you've been away.'

'You're on,' Dina said, picking up the menu sheet and fanning her smug, glistening face. 'I'll have a Francusa.'

*

Having told Dina as much as she dared about Michael and Steffi, Marta decided to call it a day. Despite all her efforts to play things straight, including her disclosure that the woman killed in the Union House explosion had been Michael's wife, Dina appeared determined to establish a romantic motive for what had happened since, and that was really pissing her off.

'Another minute of listening to your gossip-column fantasies,' Marta howled, 'and I'll go crazy.'

Dina said little during their short walk back to Central Terminus and accepted Marta's frosty embrace at the entrance to the complex without complaint. It had only just gone nine o'clock but Marta was desperate for her bed. The last few nights' sticky, suffocating heat and the drone of her ancient bedroom aircon, plus Arpad's reappearance in her dreams, had left her exhausted.

Sitting on the parked, almost empty Goval bus, Marta regretted the obfuscations and omissions in the account she had delivered to Dina: her ambiguous feelings towards the Brancusis; her having engaged Enver to put the fear of God into Arpad; her own state of mind. But then a grinning Flori Melinte had boarded the bus and sat down beside her and her introspections had been brought to an abrupt end. Having just delivered Bianca to her ex, Marta's neighbour was on a high, excited by the prospect of a whole weekend doing what *she* wanted for a change. As the bus coughed into life and rattled out of the terminus, Marta was grateful for Flori's jolly company.

'God, Bunny, am I glad to see the back of her.'

Flori's chubby arms, resting on the small backpack on her lap, vibrated like jellies in an earthquake, her hot, ample thighs pressed hard against Marta's damp cotton dress.

'I mean, I love the kid an' all that but she's been a little monster this week.'

Marta laughed. The relationship between parents and their kids had long fascinated her. All that day-to-day friction hiding such deep-seated affection.

'Yeah, my mum and me were just the same,' she told Flori. 'She was a tyrant when she was younger and I could be a real devil when I got one on me. But I'd have been horrified if anything had happened to her.'

'S'right. Me and the boys have got on so much better now they're with their dad. I just…'

Marta apologised and reached inside her handbag to retrieve the buzzing palmcom. She wasn't surprised to see that it was Steffi; she had been due to have her weekly review that afternoon with the Principal and had called Marta on her way into school, psyching herself up, telling her how well everything was going, how her grades were improving, how even the psychologist was, after all, almost bearable. For the first time, Marta had encountered the girl Michael had described so often and so proudly: optimistic, hard-working and bursting with energy… in love with life, the flip side of the tormented, hesitant teenager who had revealed herself to Marta in her bedroom at Roman House.

Marta switched off her communicator and returned it to her bag.

'Do you want me to move?' Flori said with a knowing smile.

'Oh, not you, too,' Marta snapped, mock angry. 'I've already had Dina going on all evening about men. It's just a girlfriend, OK, she can wait.'

Fifteen minutes later, back home, Marta turned up the aircon and tossed her dress, bra and knickers over the sofa en route to the bathroom, where she stood beneath a cold shower until she could breathe again. Feeling marginally more comfortable after drying herself and pulling on her dressing gown she returned to the living area and sat down on the sofa.

'Dial Steffi Brancusi,' she instructed the comscreen, absent-mindedly stroking Gypsy as she waited for the youngster to answer.

Steffi appeared, sitting at the desk in her bedroom, wearing the same wide-eyed look that had greeted Marta when they had spoken that morning.

'Hi, Marta. How was your day?'

'Oh, not bad, just the usual complaints and admin. I'll tell you what, though, I was glad I didn't have any visits to do.'

'Yeah, I must have shed like three kilos on the netball court this afternoon!'

'So what are you doing now?'

'Oh, just boring homework,' Steffi replied, shrugging her shoulders.

'So, come on then, what's with the "I won the jackpot" face?'

The teenager beamed.

'You know my review…?'

Steffi had the makings of a drama queen.

'Yes.'

'I've got a pass-out, I'm being released.'

'Wow, that's great. How did—'

'After Dr Simion had given Dad all the positive feedback he asked if I had any questions so I said could go for a sleepover at Ellie's. It's her birthday on Saturday and she's invited some of the girls from school round. Dad wasn't too comfortable with the idea and I think Dr Simion must have noticed 'cos he reminded us that the programme was about rewards as well as sanctions. Helping me regain my social confidence had to be good for my mental health, he said. Well, Dad couldn't argue with that, could he?'

Marta could see the girl was flying and was delighted for her while at the same time feeling unsettled by the note of triumph in her voice. The last thing they needed was for Michael to feel the 3D programme was driving a wedge between himself and his daughter, that wouldn't help either of them in the long run. That said, Marta had also been concerned lately about Michael's plans for Steffi once she had completed the 3D programme, his determination to 'be a good father' to his daughter, to keep her wrapped in cotton wool.

'That's fantastic news, Steffi, I'm really pleased for you. Now, you'll have to excuse me, I'm whacked.'

'OK, Marta, I'll let you know how it goes. G'night.'

'Goodnight, Steffi, sleep tight.'

TWENTY-ONE

Friday evening, Marta, Flori and Ion were preparing St Vincent's hall when a short, stocky security guard wearing Brightbeam workwear wandered in. Marta, disappointed that, for the first time in months, the company had not sent Enver, went over.

'Hi. No Enver tonight?'

The security guard grinned.

'Nah, you got me instead,' he said, holding out his hand. 'Rick Xavier. I've been posted here until twenty-two hundred.'

Marta shook the man's hand.

'Marta Ionescu. I'm the organiser.'

'Great, they said I was to ask for you.'

'OK, Rick. I'll introduce you to Ion, he'll show you the ropes.'

Marta waved her hand and the two of them headed in Ion's direction.

'So what job's the lucky Enver landed tonight then?'

'Couldn't tell you, he upped and left last weekend, no notice or nothin'.'

'Really?'

The guard leered.

'Yeah. Must've been a jealous husband.'

Marta grimaced.

*

Later, after the kids had arrived and the music was playing and the games were underway, Marta stood beneath the security light outside the hall, anxiously tapping her palmcom. She speeddialled Enver's number four times but all she got each time was the same message: 'YOU HAVE DIALLED AN INCORRECT NUMBER. PLEASE CHECK THE NUMBER AND REDIAL.' She tried the Brightbeam offices, too, but they were shut and, rather than prompt any questions, she declined the option to be put through to the company's emergency helpline.

That night, back home in bed, Marta lay awake for hours, churning over the events of the last two months, trying to decide what best to do. When daylight came and she had precious little to show for all the hours of tossing and turning, she decided that she would go to Red Way and knock on Enver's door. If that led nowhere, she would contact Brightbeam and ask if he had left a forwarding address. Other than that… Lord knows! However, there was another, unrelated matter on which she had make headway in the early hours: she was going to call Dina, apologise for her grumpiness at Grul's and tell her everything. The woman had been a good friend to her ever since she started work at the council and she deserved better. The two of them were on a day off today but, as she threw back the duvet and climbed wearily from her bed, Marta pledged to herself that she would make that call when she got back from Red Way.

*

Dina, vexed, yelled in Marta's ear, competing with the ear-splitting thump-thump-thump of dance music.

143

'What the hell were you thinking, why didn't you tell me what was going on? At least I might have persuaded you to try something else. Who knows what you've got mixed up in now? I mean, what's to say this Enver guy hasn't topped him?'

They were back at Blue, Marta's treat, her apology to her friend. But Dina's shock at Marta's revelations had grown with the turning of each sordid page and Marta was beginning to regret ever confiding in her.

'Don't be stupid,' Marta yelled back, 'he was only going to warn him off. Anyhow, what was I supposed to do, let Arpad blackmail me with his filthy mock-ups? Lose my club licence when the Council runs its annual fitness check?'

Dina shook her head, reached for the plastic tumbler on the table and took another gulp of beer. The evening wasn't turning out as either of them had planned.

'So you're sure there's no-one at the Red Way place?'

Marta shrugged.

'There was no answer; the neighbours haven't seen him in a over a week. What else can I say?'

'And Brightbeam?'

'They sounded pretty pissed off. Apparently, he'd left no forwarding address or live contact details, just not turned in one day. When they'd tried to contact him they got the same as me: number non-existent, g-mail undeliverable.'

Bemused and frustrated, the two women sat back on the upholstered wall seat, drinking their beer and watching the dancers. Suddenly, Dina nudged Marta and put her mouth to her ear.

'What's that bar called you and Psycho used to hang out at?'

'Adrian's?'

'Yeah. You could call there and ask for Arpad.'

'Are you mad? Why would I want to speak—'

'You wouldn't have to. If they say, "I'll just give him a shout," you'll know he's still around. Or if they say, "Nah, I ain't seen him for weeks," that'll tell you something else. At least that'll be one thing off your mind.'

'But they'd recognise my voice, they know me well enough.'

Dina downed another mouthful of beer and considered Marta's response.

'What about that cute barman you're always going on about? You could call him.'

Marta mulled over Dina's suggestion. True, she'd always got on well with Jotti and felt she could trust him. He'd alerted her to Arpad's foul mood the night she'd given him his marching orders, stood up for her, too, when things turned nasty. She leaned over and positioned her lips next to her friend's ear.

'I think you might be on to something. Thanks, D.'

Dina grinned smugly and sat back to continue her appraisal of the other clubgoers: the women's clothes, the men's fitness, the dancers' moves... Marta, meanwhile, rehearsed how she would contact Jotti, what she would say to him to get the information she needed without alerting his curiosity. Perhaps she could be having second thoughts about her and Arpad, perhaps—

Marta flinched when Dina elbowed her in the ribs.

'Much more competition like that and neither of us will be getting a look-in tonight.'

Marta followed her friend's gaze to the far edge of the dancefloor where... *Oh my God!* There was Steffi, clad in a tiny skirt, tight top and tall heels, her face cloaked in make-up, gyrating wildly with two much older men.

'Talk about jail bait,' Dina yelled, gleefully.

Marta was aghast and turned to her friend.

'You wondered what my angle is with Michael and his daughter. Well, you're about to find out... That's her.'

'Huh?'

Marta jumped up, marched onto the dancefloor and weaved through the crowd. Arriving before the closed-eyed Steffi she positioned herself, hands on hips, behind the teenager's nearest admirer. Steffi opened her eyes and smiled but then she spotted Marta and her mouth fell open. Marta signalled to her to follow but Steffi scowled and carried on dancing. So the older woman slipped her palmcom from her jeans and made to dial, at which point the youngster shrugged her shoulders and sashayed from the dancefloor in Marta's wake. Back at the table, Marta, fuming, pointed to the seat she had vacated next to Dina before sitting down on one of the low stools opposite.

'Dina, Steffi. Steffi, Dina.'

'Hiya, hon,' Dina shouted, enjoying the drama, wondering what would happen next.

'Hi,' the morose Steffi replied.

Marta took her wallet from her jeans, extracted a credit card and held it out to Dina.

'D'you mind, D? Would you like a drink, Steffi – a soft one?'

Steffi gave a petulant shake of the head. Dina took the card and stood up.

'Same again?'

Marta nodded.

'Thanks.'

Dina departed and Marta leaned forward menacingly.

'A sleepover at Ellie's, eh? Tell me why I shouldn't call your dad right now.'

Steffi gave Marta one of her haughty looks but said nothing.

'So you want to get thrown off the programme, prove that your dad was wrong to trust you... Plus probably lose any chance of visiting Petra inside?'

'You bitch.'

'I've been called a lot worse than that in my time, dear. Now, where's your mate?'

'I've haven't the faintest.'

Marta tapped her palmcom and Steffi's shoulders slumped.

'She went off with some guy. We agreed to meet back here at one.'

Marta checked her wristwatch. Twenty minutes. Enough time for a nice—

Two strong hands squeezed Marta's shoulders before Paolo slipped past her and sat on the seat next to an astonished Steffi.

'Hi, Marta. Mind if I introduce myself to your gorgeous friend?'

Paolo flashed Steffi a stunning smile and held out his hand.

'Paolo Gheorghiu.'

Starstruck, Steffi shook the proffered hand.

'Steffi.'

'Beautiful. Wanna dance?'

As the grinning teenagers slipped between the tables, Dina arrived back with two more beers, frowning as she planted the tumblers on the table. Marta gritted her teeth and shook her head.

'Don't ask,' she snapped.

TWENTY-TWO

Marta dialled voice only.

'Heh, Princess, what's happening?'

A spider scurried across her belly; it was wonderful to hear Jotti's voice again, so calm and reassuring.

'Crazy days. I've been put on the Union House rebuild, and that's on top of my normal job.'

'Well, you don't sound too upset about it.'

'Nah, you know me, I like to keep busy.'

'I'm sorry, Marta, *we're* pretty busy right now, too. Can I call—'

'I'll be quick, Jot. I've been trying to get hold of Arpad, has he been in lately?'

The background noise receded. It sounded as though Jotti had moved into the storeroom behind the bar.

'Not lately, no. In fact, come to think of it, I don't think I've seen him since Easter.'

'Really?'

'You know what he's like, always off on some business trip or other.'

'Sure, but three weeks?'

'Who knows? Listen, do you want me to call you if he comes in?'

'Er... Yeah, why not?'

'OK, gotta run. Byee.'

Marta put down her palmcom and ran her hand over Gypsy's fur. *What could Arpad be up to now?*

*

The days raced by during May, the Union House rebuild taking up more and more of Marta's time as she pored over architects' plans and equipment specs with Claudia Lacroix and met with her project team colleagues at twice-weekly video meetings. Combined with the increase in assessments and an explosion in customer complaints resulting from a backlog in repairs, the rebuild led to a big and welcome increase in the overtime Marta clocked up. Sadly, as Dina was also a trained assessor, the two friends saw little of each other in the weeks following their eventful night out at Blue.

Michael kept Marta updated on Steffi's progress via the occasional text, but these were becoming less frequent as Steffi's ongoing school marks remained excellent, her blood results and psychological reports positive. Fearing the dreadful consequences for both father and daughter were the teenager to be kicked off the 3D programme and expelled from school, Marta had decided early on to say nothing about Steffi's visit to Blue. But her desire to put the events of that evening behind her were abruptly demolished one Friday morning when, on the way to work, she stopped to buy some mints from Ion.

'Paolo tells us it was you who introduced him to his latest girlfriend,' he'd gushed. 'Some beauty, eh, that Steffi?'

That evening, when Paolo failed to show up at the club, Marta stood outside the hall furiously tapping her palmcom. Minutes later the beaming youth ambled down the path.

'You're a hard guy to get hold of,' Marta said, scowling.

'Sorry, Marta, it's been a busy week what with training and—'

'Don't… What's all this about you and Steffi?'

Paolo's grin faded.

'I met her from school a couple of times. We text. So what?'

'Paolo, you need to understand. She's only fifteen and very vulnerable right now.'

Paolo nodded sagely.

'Yeah, she told me all about her mum. And the 3D programme.'

'She did?'

A shriek of laughter interrupted their exchange and they stepped to one side as a gaggle of girls came down the path, yelling greetings and making doe eyes at Paolo.

'I'll cheer her up,' Paolo said after the girls had disappeared inside.

'How so?'

'We're going out tomorrow night.'

Marta could not believe what she had just heard.

'On a date?'

Paolo's next statement knocked her even further sideways.

'Sure, to the flicks. Her dad was cool.'

'You've spoken to him?'

A hint of irritation crept into Paolo's voice; he was beginning to tire of this inquisition.

'She has to be back by eleven or else. And definitely no booze.'

Marta was astonished. Why hadn't Michael – or Steffi – mentioned this to her?

'And can Mr Brancusi, who's not long buried his wife, rely on you?'

Paolo crossed himself.

'Trust me, Marta. She'll be fine.'

And with that he gave Marta a brisk, businesslike nod of the head and went inside. Marta remained where she was for a while, simmering in the hot, sticky air as she mulled over what Paolo had just told her. But the night's surprises were not yet complete.

Just ninety minutes or so later, after Marta had returned home and flopped down on the sofa to watch the end of a chat show on TV, Michael called. Switching to the coms channel she found him sitting at the desk in Sophie's study, smiling brightly and surrounded by shelves loaded with his wife's law books and certificates. After running through the niceties – Marta's work, Steffi's progress – he got to the point.

'I just wanted to check you're still off this weekend.'

'I am, and looking forward to doing sod all.'

'Well, Steffi and I wondered if you fancied a picnic tomorrow?'

'A picnic! Where?'

'Isla.'

'Where's that?'

'It's near Targu Mures. There's a small national park just off the autoroute. I'm taking the Merc out for a final run before I put her up for sale.'

Under Project Etna, the Union's massive green city initiative, non-commercial petrol vehicles had been barred from the city. Citizens wanting to keep their vehicles, and who could afford the rents, had to garage them in one of the two Parks, the huge transport interchanges built outside Caradea. Michael's beloved Mercedes was stored out at East Parks.

'What's brought this on? I mean, selling your baby?'

'Oh, it's just not the same without Soph. I used to enjoy her telling me off for pretending that I was the same young petrolhead she'd met back in Munich.'

'So now you want me to endorse your lack of green credentials?'

'Please don't feel—'

'I'm kidding, Michael, I'd love to come.'

'Right... Great.'

A sudden crash of thunder shook the apartment walls.

'Christ!' Michael exclaimed, his eyes wide. 'Did you hear that? Sounds like we're in for some rain.'

'Sounded like a plane crash,' Marta cried, catching her breath.

They paused to listen as a muted rumble followed.

'We could meet at the East Parks stop at Central Terminus, say, half-nine. If that suits.'

So much for my lie-in.

'Absolutely. But... I was going to do my shopping tomorrow. I've not got a thing in the fridge.'

'Don't worry about that, we'll take care of the food. As long as you've got your water and sun-block you'll be fine. Oh, and maybe an anorak.'

'Wow, how exciting. I've not been on a proper picnic since we moved here. By the way, what's this I hear about Steffi going on a date?'

Michael's face contorted; he was clearly embarrassed by her question.

'I'm sorry, we were going to tell you tomorrow... I'm a bit anxious, truth be told. I rather think the Principal and Steffi ganged up on me, playing the mental-health card. That sleepover at Ellie Szabo's seems to have set a precedent.'

Ah, yes, the sleepover at Ellie's...

'But Paolo's a regular at your club, I understand, and I'm impressed by his maturity.'

'Sure, but... well, I was surprised, to say the least, when he told me.'

'One thing talking with the psychologist has taught me, Marta: I can't deprive Steffi of a social life indefinitely. Somewhere along the way a parent has to take risks.'

'Yes, well, I'm sure they'll have a lovely time. I'll see you at East Parks then. Half-nine.'

'Sure. Goodnight, Marta.'

'Goodnight... END CALL.'

Marta powered-down the comscreen and sat in the half-light, trying to control her irritation. A drive out in a classic car, a picnic, proper countryside... What's not to like?

TWENTY-THREE

Marta was delighted to wake on Saturday morning and find that the storm had passed. The lightning and thunder had been awesome: searing electric flashes followed by their rumbling, crashing progeny. It was like trying to sleep through an artillery barrage. At one point during the night she had stood at the bedroom window in her pyjamas, peeping through the curtains at the illuminations. But now, with the sun lighting up the bedroom and the sound of birdsong trickling in through the vents, order had clearly been restored. The picnic was very definitely on.

Central Terminus that Saturday morning was bustling, weekend travellers streaming out to the Parks to catch a train or pick up a hire car. Marta was the first to arrive at the East Parks stop and stood to one side scrolling through the messages on her palmcom. Michael and Steffi arrived just a few minutes later, all branded walkwear and bulging backpacks.

'Check out those skinny thighs,' Steffi joshed, removing her sunglasses and looking Marta up and down.

'I'd rather have my thighs than your colour, girl. I hope you've doused yourself in factor thirty.'

The three of them laughed, unshouldered their backs and

tagged on to the back of the queue which, thankfully, was moving briskly. When Michael started talking to the man in front of him who was wearing the Dynamo away strip, Steffi murmured into Marta's ear.

'Thanks for not grassing me up.'

'Maybe I should have done. I'm not happy about you and Paolo.'

'Jesus, not you too. Why does everyone want me to be miserable?'

'No-one wants that, Steffi, but there's a lot going on in your life that needs sorting before you start dating, that's all.'

'And I thought—'

Michael turned back to face them, shaking his head.

'That chap had tickets to the Final,' he said. 'Reckons the video judge was in PSG's pocket!'

'Dad, you should have worn your longer shorts, the veins on the back of your thighs are all... Ugh.'

Michael shrugged his shoulders and looked at Marta.

'See what I have to put up with?'

'And your tummy,' Steffi continued. 'Mum used to call him *"Gespenstheuschrecke"*, Marta. Stick-insect, can you believe that?'

It was true: Michael had hovered just above 'underweight' for practically his entire married life. Sophie would get a shock if she saw him now.

'Heh, wasn't last night crazy?' Marta said, eager to move the conversation along. 'I didn't sleep more than three or four hours.'

But Steffi was determined to continue her baiting.

'Is that another of your country-girl specialities, the weather?'

Marta screwed up her face and affected an exaggerated rustic accent.

'Arrr, us country folk, we know a thing or two about nature's ways.'

'Idiot!' Steffi said, playfully thumping the older woman's shoulder.

Once on board the tram, their palmcoms swiped and backpacks stowed securely on the luggage rack, they made their way to one of the side benches and sat down in a row. While Steffi chatted excitedly with her father about their destination, Marta examined the other passengers: the families discussing their plans or watching the tele-ads, the tiny blond-haired lad wearing a kilt quizzing his parents about the trip to Grandma's. Their excitement was contagious: now that the heatwave had broken the weather was perfect for picnicking. And seeing Steffi and Michael getting along so well was the icing on the cake, a joy to witness after all the tears and heartache of recent times.

Fifteen minutes later, clear of the city limits and gliding along the East Parks autostrip, the trio's conversation turned to practical matters. Which routes would be quietest on a Saturday? Where would they find the best views? But as they neared the interchange with its jumble of workshops, warehouses and multi-storey car parks, Michael became increasingly animated.

'East and West Parks now cover over two thousand hectares between them,' he proudly informed Marta. 'Over ninety per cent of that is brownfield land recovered from the communists' defunct industrial complexes.'

Ignoring his daughter's groans and exaggerated yawns, he pressed on.

'Of course, none of this would have been possible without the billions of Euros provided by the Union. Without that cash we could never have afforded the services needed to tempt residents to vote for the trial, to abandon their cars in favour of a much-improved, much greener public transport system.'

'And no bad thing, either,' Marta replied. 'I can remember how noisy and polluted Caradea was when we first arrived.'

'Ozone and particulate levels down eighty per cent in a decade,' Steffi chimed in. 'Deaths due to chest and heart disease halved.'

Steffi smiled proudly at her father, acknowledging his affection for this place, the part he had played over the years in making it a reality.

'Yeah, I can't wait for the tram to reach Goval,' Marta enthused. 'Ditch all those stinky old boneshakers!'

Michael's stiff smile suggested that her optimism might be misplaced. After all, for months now there had been talk of further federal budget cuts. Deciding not to press the point, and with the tram entering the East Parks approach road, she took in the passing sights: the railway station with its elegant glass and iron canopy, the Park's central avenue with its recharging bays and body swap workshops, battery rental depots and vehicle disassembly plants. Minutes later the tram pulled up outside Car Park 2 and the three of them stepped down, shouldered their packs and headed for the Best-T Storage office.

Seeing the Merc standing outside on the forecourt, the scarlet paintwork washed and waxed, the alloy wheels sparkling in the sunlight, Michael was delighted.

'Great job,' he told the attendant. 'I'll try not to get her too mucky.'

Marta was no car person – growing up in Rietsa there was just the little van her father used for fetching and carrying supplies and their ancient, rickety tractor – but seeing this beautiful-looking vehicle she couldn't resist running her hand over the front wing's soft curves. After stowing the backpacks on top of the neatly folded dustsheet in the boot, the three of them climbed in, Steffi next to her father, Marta in the back.

'Great smell,' Marta said, inhaling the scent of the leather upholstery.

'Isn't it just! Now, have a listen to this.'

Michael turned the ignition key and the engine burst into life. He looked at Marta in the rear-view mirror, grinning like a cheeky kid.

'Wow, it's like our old tractor,' Marta cried.

Michael could not believe his ears.

'Your tractor?'

Steffi laughed and looked over her shoulder at Marta.

'I think you're meant to say something like it sounds like a lion purring.'

'Oh, I'm sorry, I never really got the car thing!'

Michael sighed and tapped the accelerator slightly to produce that glorious, throaty roar that had been missing from Caradea's streets for so long now. Electric cars were quieter, cleaner and far, far cheaper to run than the Merc, but how could their artificial sounds, coming from speakers set in their bumpers, ever compare with this sublime noise?

'Are we going to sit here all day, Dad?'

Michael looked across at his daughter and snorted.

'Buckle up, then. Let's hit the road.'

They pulled on their seatbelts and Michael eased the car down the driveway.

'My turn to choose the sounds,' Steffi cried, plugging her palmcom into the slot on the wood veneer dashboard.

Classic rock. LOUD.

'Can we have the music a little quieter, please, love?' Michael pleaded as they drove out onto the street.

With a glance heavenwards, his daughter turned down the volume.

Minutes later they were bowling along the Parks' outer perimeter, past the ranks of solar panels and pylons, the wind turbines revolving lazily in the breeze, past the huge bucket lorries, laden with waste destined for recyclers all over the Union. As they drove beneath the toll arch and joined the R88 heading north, Steffi looked around at Marta.

'Wait 'til you see this place. There's a forest with a big lake in the middle and a beautiful waterfall. It's magical.'

Marta smiled, pulled on her sunglasses and settled back into her seat. Steffi's sentiments boded well for their outing. And for the teenager's future wellbeing, too.

Marta stood on a rocky promontory and felt an exhilaration she hadn't experienced since leaving Rietsa. Such pure, still air, such peace. She squinted at the eagle gliding high overhead, the bird's outstretched wings stark against the fierce blue sky, then dropped her gaze to see a man swimming in the lake, a delta of glittering ripples in his wake. As she studied the swimmer's powerful crawl she felt her own muscles start to twitch, her breathing synchronise with the roll of his shoulders and hips. A familiar glow spread across her body, that combination of pride, aching muscles and taut skin that came after a hard session in the pool. And, in the early days, after making love to Arpad.

Until recently, chance connections like this had continued to depress Marta. But she was enjoying herself far too much today to allow such gloomy thoughts to dampen her spirits. After her brief crabbiness at Central terminus, Steffi's mood had improved and, on the hour-long drive, both she and her father had displayed a mounting excitement the closer they got to Isla. Steffi had even—

'Marta. MARTA.'

Marta's daydreaming was interrupted by the sound of Michael calling. She turned and looked back at the clearing where they had stopped to have their lunch and could see him waving, Steffi on her knees unpacking the picnic things. Marta returned his wave and started off down the rocky path.

*

'Great view from up there,' Marta said as she kneeled down on the groundsheet opposite Steffi. 'I saw an eagle.'

The girl looked up and frowned.

'An eagle? Are you sure it wasn't a buzzard?'

Marta laughed.

'Jeez, you city kids think you know it all. Listen, buzzards have got stumpier heads, OK? Eagles' wings and tails are longer, and their fingers—'

'OK, OK. I was only asking!'

Their laughter filled the pine-scented air.

Seeing the quantity of food the Brancusis had brought in their backpacks – meats and cheeses, pastries and plums, a seeded loaf and some raspberry jam – Marta regretted her meagre contribution: just three half-litre bottles of water and two small cartons of fruit juice. Michael and Steffi didn't seem concerned, though, nodding eagerly as Marta enthused about the things she had seen on their walk: the yellow butterflies and nervous lynx, the amazing waterfall and the pink Rhododendra carpeting the mountainside beyond.

'It's like this where we stay in Simera,' Michael said, spreading jam on his cheese. 'Endless paths and mountain streams.'

The Brancusis had talked fondly on the drive up about their annual holiday at a chalet in the Carpathians with their friends Gabriela and Vasile and their two children, Iulian and Emilia. As she took another bite of Maria's delicious bread, Marta imagined what it must have been like when the three kids were younger and Sophie was alive, walking all day, watching the kids chase one another across the meadows, playing board games after dinner...

'Cheerfulness turns dinner into a feast,' Steffi said, quoting the old man from the village who delivered the shopping to the chalet. 'Love passes through the stomach... That's how they talk up there. Weird, eh!'

'No way. My mum and aunt still talk like that.'

Michael waved his fork at his daughter.

'Country wisdom, idiot. Listen hard and you might learn something.'

'Oh yeah, Dad. Like you know all about living in a village.'

'More salad, anyone?' asked Marta.

When they had finished eating and packed away the food

containers and tubs, the cutlery, plastic plates and glasses, Steffi lay down, propped her head on her backpack and promptly dozed off. Marta, eager to make the most of their trip, suggested to Michael that they go for a walk. He agreed, adding that he'd spotted a large ant's nest on the way up; would she mind if they took a closer look? Half an hour later, having found what he was looking for, Michael took off his sunglasses, lay down on the embankment and started prodding the earth with a stick. Marta sat a little way off on a fallen tree trunk, listening to him babbling on about ants' antennae and jaws, their sting and acid sprays. In his long shorts and khaki vest, the naff baseball cap stuck on his head, he looked and sounded like an overgrown schoolkid, the class swot showing off. Yet she found it hard to begrudge his enthusiasm, his obvious love of this place. Soon afterwards Michael climbed to his feet, seemingly unaware of the damp patches on his shirt and shorts.

'Didn't the wet bother you?' Marta asked with a chuckle.

Michael looked down.

'Ha! I didn't notice,' he replied, bemused, before coming across and sitting down beside her.

Marta leant back and savoured the warmth of the sun on her face.

'Isn't this glorious? It's so good to be able to breathe again.'

'It is… By the way, I meant to ask, how are your mother and aunt doing?'

Marta was pleasantly surprised. She had known this man, what, just a couple of months, yet here he was showing an interest in her family, one subject that Arpad never touched on.

'Loving having their curtains and windows open again. Mum's like a different woman, no more grumbling about being buried alive.'

He was such a nice guy, so down to earth despite the important job and classy apartment. He treated her with respect, too: none of those quips about her job, her accent or eating habits. Sitting there in the sunshine, Marta supposed Michael must have felt a similar contentment, for he was soon telling her all about his latest meeting at the Bishop's office, going over the final plans for Sophie's memorial service. The re-telling clearly wasn't easy for him and his voice quivered at times. Despite this, he seemed genuinely amused by some of the diplomatic arm-wrestling between the UES and Diocesan administrators.

'They were so focussed on looking after their organisations' own interests that Sophie was becoming sidelined. So I thumped the table and asked them: "Just what is it we're supposed to be commemorating here?"'

After that Michael fell silent for a while and Marta let him be. At length, he turned to her, a sombre look on his face.

'I'd appreciate your advice, Marta. There's something that's been bothering me all week.'

'Sure. Fire away.'

'It's to do with Steffi's social re-integration.'

'Why don't you just tell me?' she said gently.

He nodded and took a deep breath.

'The day after her sleepover at Ellie's we were chatting about school over supper. All of a sudden she asks me why we christened her Steffi. I wondered if this was another of her tests, you know how she likes to push the boundaries...'

Marta nodded.

'...Anyway, I reminded her that her mum was a great lover of tennis, a great player, too, at uni. It was her idea that we name our daughter after Steffi Graff, the famous German champion. "Sure, sure, I remember all that," she said, before asking why we hadn't chosen Ana Bogdan, say, or Sorana Cîrstea.'

'Tennis players?'

Michael smiled and nodded.

'I explained, as patiently as I could, that it had nothing to do with the player's nationality, that her mother wanted to name her after someone she admired. Steffi knows Sophie's views on the dangers of nationalism; she's heard the lecture often enough. Anyway, then she tells me she wants to change her name, to honour one of "our people". I was getting pretty riled at this point, I can tell you, but on she went, insisting that before long all that would be left of our country would be a bunch of museums for the tourists and folk music recordings on the grid. Finally, she looks me in the eyes and says, "Where's our dignity as a nation, Dad? Where are our heroes?" Then up she gets and waltzes off to her bedroom. I was stunned, Marta, I couldn't believe what I was hearing. Where did all this nonsense come from?'

Michael paused for breath – the re-telling was clearly getting to him – and Marta recalled the chauvinistic sentiments Steffi had voiced that night in her bedroom.

'Has she ever spoken like this before?' she asked innocently.

'Not really. I mean, she's a bright girl who likes to challenge things. But usually she speaks in academic, theoretical terms. What was so different this time round was how personal it all seemed, how she was clearly experiencing some deep and very disturbing feelings.'

Michael studied Marta's face as though searching for clues.

'So what do you think? Should I tell the Principal?'

Marta paused for thought; this wasn't straightforward. She wanted to avoid adding fuel to the flames, too.

'I think I'd want to know more. Who is she speaking to? Are the thoughts and feelings she's expressing her own or is she acting as someone else's mouthpiece? And does this have anything to do with Petra's being locked up?'

Michael nodded but Marta could see the subject was causing him considerable unhappiness.

'Look. I've got one or two contacts in the youth education service. Let me ask around, get some ideas, some options, maybe. The last thing you want is Steffi getting kicked off the programme and having to move school. It all seems to be going so well lately.'

Michael smiled awkwardly.

'Thanks, Marta, I'd appreciate that.'

*

It was near to two o'clock when they finally headed back up the path. As they walked along in silence, absorbing the sounds and smells, Marta silently thanked the tall man at her side for bringing her to this wonderful place. Arriving back at the clearing they found Steffi sprawled over the groundsheet and still asleep, her mouth open to the sky.

'Your shoulders are very red, Chickpea,' Michael said, shaking his daughter gently. 'You need to put more spray on.'

Steffi opened her eyes and looked up at her father, smiling contentedly.

'Sit up,' Marta told her, picking up the bottle of sun-block. 'I'll do your back.'

As Marta applied the spray Steffi looked up at her father.

'It reminds me of the last time we were up in Simera, Dad,' she said. 'Do you remember how everything that weekend seemed so incredibly sharp and detailed?'

'I do. All that light in the thin mountain air.'

Steffi looked over her shoulder at Marta.

'We walked for hours along forest tracks, the sound of trickling water never far away.'

'Steff led the way,' Michael continued, 'checking her compass and telling us which fork to take, teaching us all about terminal moraines and hanging valleys.'

The two of them fell silent, contemplating their memories of that day, Sophie's last visit to their friends' mountain chalet. Witnessing the scene, Marta felt her skin prickle. The two of them were getting there, she could see that; they were slowly hauling themselves out of the pit.

They had stayed at Isla longer than expected. Fortunately, the autoroute was flowing freely.

'What time do you think we'll get back, Dad?'

Michael looked across at Steffi and smiled. She was clearly getting excited about meeting Paolo.

'Around five, love. Don't worry, you'll have plenty of time to pretty yourself up.'

Steffi snorted and flicked her father's hand resting on the gear stick. Marta caught Michael's eyes in the rear-view mirror and, for a brief moment, neither looked away.

After dropping off the Merc at the storage company and taking the tram back to Caradea, the trio arrived in Central Terminus just after five-thirty. As Marta's bus went from the outdoor ranks on the far side of the complex they said their goodbyes at the tram stop.

'Let me know how it goes,' Marta said, giving the teenager an extra hug for luck.

'I will,' Steffi promised, her newly tanned face enhancing her dazzling smile.

'Thanks for a great day, Michael,' Marta said, as they exchanged a farewell kiss.

He held her just that little bit longer, like he wanted her to know.

TWENTY-FOUR

Back in Goval, Marta called round to see how her mother and aunt were keeping.

'Mercy me!' Aunt Lisha cried, inspecting Marta's legs. 'I bet you had all the men whistling.'

'Not as many as I'd like,' Marta replied, dropping her backpack on the floor. 'I've just got back from Isla, it was so beautiful.'

'So I've heard. Don't tell your mum that, though, or she'll be going on about home for hours!'

Marta laughed.

'So, how's she been today? She sounded almost cheerful first thing.'

'Why don't you go and see for yourself?'

Marta walked down the hall, heartened by the sight of sunlight spilling in once more, the peace now all the aircon units were no longer running at max. She got an even more pleasant surprise, though, when she entered the living room and came face to face with her mother emerging from the kitchen. The old lady's movements were as stiff and tentative as ever, but her breathing had clearly improved dramatically and her eyes had regained that familiar glint of defiance.

'Heh, Mama, you're looking great.'

'Hello, dear…' They kissed. 'Yes, it looks like you'll have to wait a little longer yet to get a hold of your inheritance!'

Marta grinned and stroked her mother's arm as she eased herself into her chair next to the dining table. The gloom and doom of recent days had not suited this gnarled survivor.

'That's the spirit, Mama. Thank God for the storm, eh?'

'Allelujah,' Aunt Lisha called from the kitchen where she had gone to made some tea.

Marta stayed with the pensioners for a half hour or so, sitting on the settee next to her aunt and telling them all about her outing: the beautiful scenery, her friend's old petrol car, some of the things Michael had told her about the Parks. She noticed that her mother did not smoke and hoped that her recent health scare had finally convinced her to quit. When she was satisfied that everything was OK, she finished her drink and got up to leave. They tried to persuade her to stay for a second cup but she was adamant.

'Gypsy will be crawling up the walls,' she told them.

After embracing her mother and telling her once more how pleased she was to see her looking so well, Marta walked down to the front door with Lisha, picked up her backpack and kissed her aunt goodbye. Once outside, the apartment door clunked firmly shut, she almost skipped down the sour-smelling corridor. Seeing them both looking so much better than the previous week, the apartment back to relative normality, had lifted an enormous weight from her shoulders.

Back home, Marta opened the high window in the kitchen to let in some air and emptied out her backpack, telling Gypsy all about her wonderful day as she lined up the empty water bottles, binned the used cartons and unrolled and hung up her cagoule. It was only when she got to the point in the story where they had collected the car – and Michael had spent more than her monthly food bill on a tank of petrol – that Marta realised her old friend had not greeted her in his usual, impatient way. Horrified at the thought that she might have shut him in somewhere and recalling the trail of shit over her duvet the last time she had shut him in the bedroom, she dashed through to the hall. But the bedroom and bathroom doors were both open and there was no sign of him under the bed or in the wardrobe, nor beneath the dirty clothes in her laundry basket. Where the hell was he?

Her anxiety levels rocketing, Marta wandered back to the kitchen, trying to picture her precise movements from the time she woke up and got out of bed to the time she left the apartment. Did she feed Gypsy before or after she showered? Had he been on the sofa or in his bed when she'd set out for the bus? Was there any chance he could have slipped out behind her? *Think, girl, think – there has to be an obvious answer!* Back in the kitchen she checked the dishes on Gypsy's mat, the large glazed Me-ow one licked clean from breakfast, its smaller, pale blue version still half full of water. Then she inspected the tray next to the bin and counted three tidy mounds of litter. She had cleaned and refilled the tray before leaving which meant he couldn't possibly have escaped behind her. He was probably watching her this very moment from some hidey hole, taking great delight in all the upset he was causing.

'Gypsy, you little bastard, you come here right now!'

Two steps and she was across at the fridge, intending to pour herself a large glass of wine, sit down and think this whole thing through. But when she opened the door and saw the ball of black fur curled up on her vegetable board her heart exploded. There lay Gypsy, two empty, bloodied sockets in his face, on the shelf below a glass plate bearing two coloured beads sitting in an oily, blood-flecked pool. And then she read the note propped against the olive jar – 'AN EYE FOR AN EYE, TWO FOR YOUR CHEATING' – and, clinging to the fridge, lowered her head and vomited.

*

167

Back in the apartment, Michael exhaled loudly and let his body relax. The frantic excitement of the last hour, viewing and pronouncing on Steffi's hastily assembled parade of casualwear, had exhausted him. Seeing her sitting in the back of the taxi had made it all worthwhile, though, her blonde hair down across her shoulders, her suntanned face glowing against the embroidered white silk of her mother's favourite blouse. Tonight was going to be very special, he was certain of it, though when his palmcom started to vibrate that conviction quickly disappeared. What on earth could she have forgotten now? But when he took out the device and saw that it was Marta calling his irritation was immediately swamped by a soaring hope. Maybe she, too, had felt something today. Perhaps, like him, she couldn't bear to wait until next week to talk. The moment he pressed 'Receive', though, and saw the distraught look on Marta's face, the tears in her eyes, he knew that that was not why she had called.

'Michael, you've got to help me,' she cried, the picture wobbling in her shaking hand.

'What is it, what's happened?'

'It's Gypsy, I found him… In the fridge.'

Suddenly the little screen was filled with a close up of a coffee jar, behind it two pale, cracked tiles. She had dropped her palmcom but he could still hear the sound of her wailing.

'Marta, can you hear me? Marta?'

There was a scrabble, the sound of the communicator being picked up once more. Then her face reappeared on the screen, blotchy and glistening.

'Come now, second floor,' was all she said before hanging up.

Michael dropped his palmcom on the hall table and dashed into the bedroom. Seconds later he returned, pulling on a jacket and zipping up his chinos. Grabbing his palmcom he dialled the last number he had called, the A-Line taxi company that just minutes ago had collected Steffi.

'Hello, A-Line? Yes, Roman House, straightaway, it's urgent… No, that was my daughter, I want another one… Right away!'

*

Michael marched across the lobby, feverishly wondering whether or not to call his daughter. He decided that he would hold off for now, at least until he had found out what was going on with Marta.

'Mr Brancusi? Can I help you, sir? Is everything all right?'

'Gyula. No, it's… I'm sorry, a friend's had some kind of accident, I need to get over there.'

It was at that point that Michael realised he had no idea where in Goval Marta lived. Stepping into the security vestibule he tapped her name into his palmcom, hoping to find an address. But the only answer that came back, whichever search form he used, was a 'number not-listed' notice.

'Fuck, fuck, FUCK!'

Gyula had followed him outside onto the pavement and promptly stepped forward.

'If it's an address you need, sir, I know someone who may be able to help. If you'll permit me?'

Michael looked up and down Nastase. There was no sign of an A-Line taxi so he nodded to the concierge.

'It's Ms Ionescu, Gyula. She lives somewhere in Goval.'

'First name?'

'Marta, Marta Ionescu.'

Whatever he was thinking, Bokros did not show it. He walked calmly over to the kerb and stood with his back to Michael, palmcom to his ear, muttering. Moments later he was back.

'Block 46, Apartment 2c,' he said, his face inscrutable. 'Just off Meresti Avenue North.'

'I owe you, Gyula,' Michael said, inputting the address directly onto gridmap. 'Thank you.'

It took the taxi a good twenty minutes to reach Goval, despite Michael's frequent urgings. Along the way he tried repeatedly to contact Marta but without any success. All the time her words were going round and round in his head, compelling him to try and imagine what could have happened. Could her mother be ill again, or worse? Had the problem ex she had told him about shown up? What had she meant about the cat being in the refrigerator? Whatever it was, there was no doubt in his mind. She had turned to him for assistance and he would do all he could to help her.

When they entered the estate proper and drove down Meresti, Michael's spirits plummeted. There was no transport depot in Goval so he rarely ventured out this way. He had forgotten just how depressing the place was with its row upon row of drab communist-era apartment blocks, its badly pot-holed roads and vandalised street signs. Why hadn't the council just swept the place away rather than selling it to Marta's employers? The reason, he knew well enough, was that the city could not afford to replace this huge estate with more modern housing. Seeing it now, he doubted whether VisionPlace could either.

They pulled up at a junction and a hooded youth loitering on the corner hurled his drink can at the taxi. Michael and the driver ducked, to the obvious delight of the yob and his jeering, slack-shouldered mates. Fortunately, the can was empty and bounced harmlessly off the side window and into the road. For the increasingly agitated driver, though, that was irrelevant; he accelerated away hard before the lights had changed. Further down the road he pulled in behind a stationary bus and hurriedly checked his route screen.

'I can't wait, mister, it's too dangerous round here.'

Their eyes met in the rear-view mirror. Michael could have brought up the fact that he had an account with the company, that he was an important customer. But he did not want to risk alienating this man; right now he was the only ally he had.

'I'll give you fifty,' he said, 'if you drive around awhile, until I know whether or not I need a return.'

'Cash?'

'Cash.'

The driver looked over his shoulder.

'OK, mister, but fifteen minutes max. OK?'

'OK.'

They turned into a side street bordered by apartment blocks on the right and a playground on the left. Behind the battered chain link fence some youths were playing football. The taxi slowed to a stop and the driver nodded towards the nearest block, a faded '46' printed over its entrance. Michael's heart was racing; he had never done anything like this before. He was always the studious one at school; he never bunked off or got into trouble. It suddenly occurred to him that this whole situation could be a set-up, that Marta had lured him here so that some unseen accomplices could ambush him and make off with his wallet and cards. Taking a deep breath he logged the driver's contact number, opened the door and stepped out.

'Fifteen minutes, mister.'

'Right,' Michael said, trying to control his adrenaline-filled limbs.

The taxi drove away, leaving him standing all alone by the side of the road, listening to the young footballers' calls and curses, a man shouting angrily in the distance. Even the air in this soulless place smelt bad, of chemicals and exhaust fumes, waste that, most days of the year, never troubled his part of town. Having tried and failed to contact Marta one final time he crossed the road and walked briskly towards the building's shadowy entrance.

There were no lifts in the block and so, reluctantly, nervously, he climbed the poorly lit stairs. Fortunately, the walkway up on the second floor was open-sided, providing a welcome relief from the stinking stairwell. It was cleaner, too: at least up here the inhabitants appeared to know how to use a brush. In a matter of seconds he found Flat 2c – the third door along – and pressed the bell. When there was no answer, he rapped on the neighbouring window. The blind was down but there was a light on inside. He rang again and thumped the door hard. Whatever had happened in there, he hoped he wasn't too late. Then he heard the sound of bolts being slid and a chain rattling, and he watched anxiously as the door opened slowly and Marta's frightened eyes appeared around its edge.

'Did anyone follow you, Michael?'

Her quavering voice and bloodshot eyes unnerved him, as did her question. Whatever had happened to the confident, happy woman he had left at Central Terminus not two hours ago?

'No, the only people I saw were some kids over in that playground.'

'OK, come in. Quick.'

Marta opened the door wide and Michael stepped inside. She was still wearing the clothes she had worn for the picnic but had nothing on her feet. Whilst she fixed the chain and bolts he cast a quick eye over the pokey kitchen/living space with its old fashion, well-worn furniture, its unpleasant, sour smell. When she had finished locking up, Marta briskly turned and launched herself at him, flinging her arms around his waist and bursting into tears. Shocked by the sheer force of her misery, he held her tight and felt her bony back, her shaking body.

'He's coming for me, I know it. He's killed Gypsy and he's going to do the same to me.'

'Ssh,' Michael said, stroking Marta's hair and trying to calm her. 'We haven't got long so let me ask the questions, OK?'

Marta nodded and he looked over her head at the pool of vomit on the floor in front of the refrigerator, the splashes up the appliance's clean white front.

'Who is *he*?'

'My ex, Arpad.'

'How can you be certain it was him?'

She pointed at a neatly hand-printed card lying on the worktop: '*An eye for an eye, two for your cheating.*'

'Have you called the police?'

He felt her body stiffen.

'No, no, I don't want them involved.'

'OK, OK. I won't—'

'He must have got in here while I was out and—'

Her body was wracked by a further bout of sobbing.

'Oh, my boy, my poor darling boy. He's coming back for me, Michael, he knows about us and he's going to finish it.'

She pulled some kitchen roll from her pocket and wiped her eyes and Michael pondered her words. *He's blinded Gypsy... He knows about us.*

'Marta... Marta, listen. Where is Gypsy now?'

She opened her mouth but just gulped up at him like a stranded fish. This was killing her.

'I... I took his basket into my... bedroom and lay him in there...'

Michael's mind worked fast as he calculated the options and reached his conclusion.

'OK. There's a taxi outside that will leave without us in... eight minutes if we don't get a move on. I want you to grab a bag and pack some clothes and come with me. You'll be safe at Roman House; you'll be able to take your time to decide what to do for the best. Are you alright with that?'

Marta, her head still on his chest, nodded. Then she was gone.

*

Marta lay on the soft leather sofa, staring up at the ceiling and thinking about Gypsy in his basket on the bed, his lifeless body wrapped in her white swimming towel like some ancient mummy. She longed to hold him again, to feel his fur against her face and hear his contented purr. But all she felt was the void caused by his loss, fast filling again with that gagging, pinching terror, the legacy of Arpad's brutal message. In an effort to console herself she thought once more about her promise that she would come back soon for him, the poem she had read aloud through a veil of tears. She had only got as far as the second verse of 'Motherland' when the doorbell had rung.

Michael's appearance had given her hope, had demonstrated that she was not alone. Here was someone prepared to come to her assistance, to shoulder some of the burden as well as the worry and the fear. She had not needed convincing to leave the apartment though; whatever Michael had suggested in the end, she had already made up her mind. But she had not thought beyond her escape and had little idea where to go or what she would need. All she cared about was surviving, surviving in order to get revenge for Gypsy.

Listening to Michael pottering about in the kitchen area, comfortable and certain back in his own world, Marta's line of thinking veered off in a new, disturbing direction. Had she, in focussing on her own escape and safety, put Michael and Steffi in danger? If Arpad was unable to get to her, might he be tempted to go for Mama or Aunt Lisha? The thought made her shudder and she decided that she would call her mother and warn her to... To what? She and Aunt Lisha did not have the comfort of twenty-four-hour porterage, of CCTV and security vestibules. They were, like her, women alone in this sick, cruel world.

She felt a hand on her shoulder and looked up to see Michael leaning over her.

'Your chocolate,' he said, placing the beaker on the huge coffee table before sitting down on the sofa next to her feet.

She leaned over and picked up her drink and blew on the hot, foamy liquid. He looked at her and smiled softly, a slight frown on his forehead. For such a talkative man he could be very quiet at times… His offer had come out of the blue and she had seized it like an exhausted swimmer desperately reaching for a float. Roman House was secure and Goval felt a world away here. Maybe that was why, the moment they were safe inside Michael's apartment, behind that reinforced steel door, she had not struggled when he had kissed her, had not minded being led into the living room and lowered gently onto the nearest sofa, feeling the tug of his hand on her tracksuit bottoms. They had fucked with a desperate urgency, a shared determination to obliterate all the violence and grief that had swamped their recent lives. When it was over she had collapsed beside him, hot and breathless, and welcomed the light touch of his hand on her thigh and face.

'I hadn't planned for that to happen,' he'd said, anxiously. 'That wasn't why I suggested you come back here.'

'I believe you,' she'd told him, reaching out to muss his already messed-up hair. 'Don't look so worried, you might make me think you're regretting it.'

*

After Michael had kissed her goodnight, Marta lay in bed in the dark, weeping into her pillow, her distress rekindled by the thought of Gypsy's suffering and abandonment. Mingled in with these gloomy thoughts, however, were memories of the day's many happy moments: Steffi's obvious delight at being in Isla, the awesome waterfall, that eagle flying high overhead… At one point Marta felt Michael's breath on her neck, warm and close, as though he was lying next to her again. Poor Michael, his face had been such a picture of surprise…

THUD! Marta's journey in limbo land was shattered by the sound of the front door being slammed and Steffi sobbing hysterically, then

Michael pounding down the hall to remonstrate with his daughter. Marta reached for her palmcom; it was 12.38: her young friend was over ninety minutes late, no wonder there were tears. Gradually, the whispers and stifled cries receded, although they soon started up again once the unhappy couple were behind the living-room door. This second round of exchanges continued for several minutes – Steffi's shrill, disturbed cries; Michael's deep, measured responses – until Marta heard the sound of heavy footsteps coming back down the hall and Michael creeping into her room.

'Marta, are you awake?' he asked, crossing to the bed. 'I'm sorry to disturb you but something's happened, something serious. Would you mind joining us in the living room?'

His voice sounded oddly formal, as though he was back at work. There was no sign of any anger or agitation in it; rather, a patent but controlled anxiety. Marta, wearing just her bra and knickers, slipped from the bed and pulled on her tracksuit top.

'What is it? What's happened?'

He reached out and touched her cheek and she caught his face in the light from the hall. She had never seen him looking so worried; he was practically grey.

'She wants to speak to you… Sorry, I need to get back.'

'OK, I'll be right down, just give me a second.'

He turned and left the room and Marta pulled on her bottoms. Then, after using the toilet in Steffi's bathroom next door, she rushed along to the living room. There she found Steffi in a shocking state: mascara running down her cheeks, her hair dishevelled, her blouse and trousers stained and ripped. She was perched on the edge of one of the sofas, her hands clasped tightly in front of her as though she was praying. Michael was sitting beside her, his arm around her shoulders. As Marta crossed the room Steffi looked up.

'Paolo's dead,' she said matter-of-factly. 'They killed him.'

Marta suddenly felt very cold, her legs weak. She sat down next to Steffi and took the girl's badly scratched hand in hers.

'Dead?'

Steffi raised her red, swollen eyes and looked directly at her.

'It was horrible,' she cried. 'Horrible.'

A clutch of questions raced through Marta's mind but she could see the girl was in shock. She needed to avoid putting her under any more pressure.

'It's OK, Chickpea, you're safe now,' Michael murmured.

Marta caught Michael's eye.

'Michael, could you fetch the duvet from Steffi's bed, please? She feels very cold.'

With Michael gone, Steffi turned to Marta, her eyes wide and wet.

'Oh, Marta, I've been so stupid. I'll go to prison for this, it'll finish my dad off.'

'Hey, shh, hush now. One step at a time.'

Marta stroked the girl's back and handed her more paper handkerchiefs from the box on the table. Steffi wiped her eyes and blew her nose.

'It was like they knew we were coming. Like they were waiting for us.'

Michael returned with the duvet and, while he fussed around his daughter, draping the covering over Steffi's legs and tucking it in beneath her arms, Marta thought about what the girl had said. Who were they? And what had alerted them? When Michael was done he sat down again but Steffi was still shaking, the words tumbling once more from her lips.

'There were two of them, one stamping on his head, the other hitting him with a pole. They were going mad, it was...'

Steffi shook her head and dabbed her eyes. Marta caught the look on Michael's face, the incomprehension and horror.

'Shh,' she said, holding Steffi closer and mouthing 'water' to her father.

Marta had entered another world, numb and hazy, where certainty had evaporated and questions flooded her mind. Michael brought over the water and they watched Steffi take the glass in both hands and gulp down half the contents. When the teenager was done, Marta took the glass and placed it on the coffee table.

'Steffi. Where is Paolo now?'

Steffi looked at Marta, dazed.

'We were in Almany—'

'Almany?' Michael yelled, jumping to his feet. 'What on earth were you doing out there?'

Marta shook her head angrily at him. No.

'Don't be afraid, Steffi, just answer your father.'

Steffi shivered and started sobbing again.

'Paolo said he'd show me where the illegals lived,' she wailed. 'One of his mates drove us out there in his taxi... We were just going to give them a little fright. It was only meant to be a joke.'

Marta stepped in again; she needed to know.

'So, is there anything we can do to help Paolo right now?'

Steffi pondered the question.

'He just went quiet and stopped trying to defend himself. Then the police came and the men ran off.'

Over the next fifteen to twenty minutes, Marta gently teased out the story, trying to keep Steffi as calm as possible while piecing together what had happened. Motives and background were unimportant for now; her priority was to find out if there was any chance that Paolo might still be alive... According to Steffi, she, Paolo and his mate Kam had driven out to the Almany district in Kam's taxi to show Steffi where the so-called 'illegals' – undocumented migrants – were housed. Concealed in a dark alley behind the Welcome Home, they had spied on four young 'foreign' women in the hostel's kitchen, merrily drinking wine. Someone – Paolo or Kam – had thrown a bottle which had smashed against the back wall of the house and, having cheerily witnessed the alarm this had caused, the trio turned and ran. But two men had emerged from nowhere and chased after them and, when Paolo tripped, the men fell on him, kicking and beating him without mercy. Steffi, hiding in some nearby bushes, had witnessed the whole appalling incident.

'It was dreadful,' she cried. 'He was screaming for help.'

At this point in the telling Steffi froze, clearly too distressed to continue. Marta handed her the glass of water and, stunned by what she had heard, watched her drink down the remainder. What on earth had possessed these bright, intelligent kids to do such a thing?

Michael, who had been pacing the room and muttering to himself, stopped before them.

'We're going to have to call the police,' he said. 'They'll find out sooner or later. Someone will have seen the two of you together, clocked the taxi, whatever. Better to get in first and tell them the truth.'

Marta felt Steffi stiffen.

'No, Dad, we can't.'

Michael bristled.

'Why not?'

Steffi stared at her father, her mind working overtime.

'Because one of the men… It was that cop who interviewed us. The captain.'

Michael dropped down on the arm of the sofa, a look of disbelief on his face. Marta seized Steffi's hand.

'You mean Captain Pal? The guy leading the hunt for the Union House bombers?'

Steffi nodded.

Marta sat back and closed her eyes, allowing the events of recent weeks to run through her mind. She saw Arpad's photograph of Ludmilla Fedoruk sitting in a car with Sophie Brancusi, found herself up on the roof of Roman House inspecting the Brancusis' skylight. And all of a sudden she realised what had been troubling her about that assessment these last few weeks.

'It was like they knew we were coming. Like they were waiting for us.'

The aim of the break-in had not been to steal anything from the apartment; it had been to plant something in it.

*

Appalling as Steffi's story was, the revelation concerning Pal left Marta little time to grieve for Paolo. Her focus now was on what they should do. Assuming that the apartment really had been bugged, whoever was responsible would have heard Steffi's account and know that she was a witness to at worst murder, at best a brutal, probably life-changing assault. By a serving police officer. If Pal had anything to do with the bugging, he would be after them. If it wasn't Pal, whoever was responsible had performed a criminal act and might wish to secure the Brancusis' silence. Either way, Marta knew she had to get the couple to a place of safety. Gesturing to Steffi and her astonished father, she put her finger to her lips then seized the remote, tuned the comscreen to the first rock music channel she could find and turned the volume up high.

'Don't speak,' she whispered in their ears. 'The apartment's bugged.'

By now Steffi was pretty zoned out, drained by the evening's grotesque events. Michael, however, looked at Marta as though she had lost her mind, shrugging his shoulders and mouthing, 'What?' repeatedly. But Marta hadn't got time for questions. Telling Michael that she was going to check out Steffi's story, and urging him to keep his daughter quiet, she left the Brancusis huddled together on the sofa and walked briskly along to Steffi's bedroom. After grabbing the notepad and pencil lying on the teenager's desk, she went next door to the guestroom, sat down on the bed and plugged in her earphones before scrolling through the local news channel on her palmcom. She soon found the headline she was looking for:

'MURDER IN ALMANY' – and, while gazing at the images

on the screen – the cop cars parked across the street, the officers in forensic coveralls emerging from a taped-off, floodlit alley – listened to the accompanying report.

'...reported by a local resident at around ten forty-five. The cause of the dispute and identity of the assailants is, so far, unclear.'

The camera panned round to settle on the female reporter's face.

'If you've just switched on, we're coming to you live from Almany where there has been a disturbance outside the northern sector Welcome Home. One person, a Caucasian male, is known to have died.'

Marta felt sick. The spark of hope she had nurtured since hearing Steffi's story, that Paolo might have survived, had been extinguished. Of course, the 'Caucasian male' could be someone else but that now seemed very much like wishful thinking. Swallowing back the tears, she returned the earphones to her backpack, took out the disposable phone she had retrieved from her mother and started thumbing a message.

*

Back in the living room, Marta sat down on the coffee table in front of her friends and attempted a reassuring smile. Michael grimaced while Steffi, barely awake, managed only the faintest of nods. Placing the notepad on her knees Marta wrote carefully, in capitals:

'NO SPEAK. PACK BAG FOR 2/3 DAYS. WEAR JACKET. BRING ALL CASH YOU HAVE AND KEYS TO MERC. BE QUICK. I HAVE TO MAKE A CALL.'

Having secured Michael's assent, Marta nodded her thanks, closed the pad and headed off. Michael and Steffi followed her down the hallway and watched her take the keycard from its insert and open the front door. Glancing over her shoulder, Marta tapped her wristwatch and waved them away. Then, as father and daughter scuttled off to their rooms, she stepped out into the corridor and pulled the door to behind her.

Barely ten minutes later Michael emerged from his bedroom to find Marta standing by the hall table, her palmcom sitting beneath the lamp, her backpack – packed – on the floor. When he walked across she held up the notepad.

'LEAVE PALMCOM HERE. CAN BE TRACKED.'

He nodded. She was leaps and bounds ahead of him.

'LEAVE COMSCREEN AND LIGHTS ON. NO TALKING UNTIL I SAY.'

He nodded again and Marta checked her wristwatch. Frowning, she strode off to Steffi's room, reappearing seconds later dragging the wretched teenager by the arm, her still-open backpack hanging from her shoulder. After having the notepad held up in front of her eyes, Steffi stepped back and raised her hands in surrender before reluctantly handing over her palmcom. She was starting to look more than a little afraid of this new, fiercer version of their friend. Marta pulled on her backpack and signalled Michael and Steffi to do the same. Then, gesturing for the two of them to follow, she led the way down the hall and out into the corridor. After closing the apartment door she handed Michael the keycard and strode down to the fire escape at the far end of the corridor, the bewildered Brancusis in her wake. Once inside she led the way up the dimly lit staircase, Steffi following and Michael bringing up the rear.

'Where are—'

Marta swung round abruptly and thrust her hand over Steffi's mouth before delivering more of the familiar lip-tapping. Then she smiled, cocked her head roofwards and mouthed, 'Come on.'

As she climbed the steps, the adrenaline flooding her body, Marta went through the plan. The first stage had been successfully completed: she had got the Brancusis safely out of their apartment. Now she could only hope that the keypad code she had watched Bokros use for the rooftop exit had not been changed. The last thing she wanted was to trigger the alarm and alert the concierge and maybe the police to their presence on the roof. The transport was sorted and Tony was checking out the destination she had in mind. She just needed to get the Brancusis clear of the building and out of the open and then she could relax… They reached the exit at the top of the staircase and Marta tapped the code into the keypad. It worked! Pushing down on the bar, she stepped out onto the roof and waved for the others to follow.

Peering at the forest of aerials and satellite dishes, the cables and pipes barely visible beneath the moon's slim crescent, Marta knew they would have to be careful where they stepped. She reached out to take Steffi's hand and motioned Michael to do likewise. But no sooner had she leaned forward and peered around the corner of the block than she hopped briskly back into the shadow and tugged Steffi and Michael back inside the stairwell, yanking the door to behind them. Within seconds they could hear and feel the low hum of a drone as the machine hovered overhead, its sweeping searchlights filtering beneath the stairwell door. Marta watched and listened, trying to discern what the object was up to. Steffi looked petrified and buried her face in Michael's chest. And then, as quickly as it had arrived, the drone was gone.

*

They came down from the roof via the fire escape at the far end of the block and lingered in an unlit alley amongst the bins and flattened boxes. After telling Michael and Steffi to keep their voices down, Marta took herself off to the roadside entrance to keep a lookout for Tony. A few minutes later his battered taxi drew up at the kerbside, its petrol exhaust spewing grey clouds. With a wave from Marta, the Brancusis abandoned their hiding place, hurried across the sidewalk and tossed their bags into the boot. As the trio scrambled into the rear of the vehicle Tony took a last pull on his cigarette and tossed it out of the window.

'Thanks, Tony,' Marta said, sliding in next to Steffi and pulling the door shut.

'No problem,' came the reply over the intercom, deep and calm. 'The missus was pissed but she soon came round when I told her it was a cash fare!'

Marta laughed.

'Tony, this is Michael and Steffi, the friends I told you about.'

'Hi, guys,' the driver said, checking his rear-view mirror before pulling out.

'Hi,' Michael said, unimpressed by what passed as a taxi in Goval.

Steffi, her mouth sagging, her eyelids fluttering, nodded weakly. The poor girl was fading fast. Marta pulled a bottle of water from her satchel and offered it to her but Steffi declined. So Marta passed it to Michael, who unscrewed the cap and gulped down several mouthfuls.

'Still East Parks, yeah?' Tony asked.

'Yep,' Marta replied. 'Best-T Storage.'

'Gotcha.'

Michael returned the bottle to Marta, frowning, and leaned forward.

'Er, excuse me, you know you're heading west.'

'Listen – Mike, ain't it? – leave the driving to me, OK? I know what I'm doin'. You worry about keeping these two little ladies safe.'

Michael opened his mouth and Marta readied herself to intervene. But he must have realised that he wasn't in the strongest of bargaining positions and decided, instead, to sit back in his seat.

The gravelly voice came over the intercom again.

'OK, listen up. No-one's carrying a palmer, right?'

'No,' Marta replied. 'We left them in the apartment just like you said, switched on.'

'Good. Now, in a half k I'm going to slow down and I want you to get rid of your disposable, Marta.'

Marta yelped.

'Heh, that cost me fifty, Tony, why—'

'You paid cash?'

'No, I—'

'You swiped, right? So some server somewhere will know what credit you have on that phone and will be able to track it. And you.'

'OK, OK,' Marta snapped. 'I get the message!'

'Ah!' Michael said. 'So that's why we're heading West.'

Tony shrugged his shoulders.

'Sure, why else?' he said, before leaning across and slipping a fresh disposable into the drawer behind him. 'Don't worry, this one's clean. But emergencies only, Marta, right? And watch what you say. No names or places.'

'Don't worry,' Marta said, pocketing the phone. 'I know the drill.'

Michael's frustration was growing; he wasn't used to not being in control.

'Are you going to tell me where we're going now?'

The taxi slowed.

'I'm turnin' here, Marta,' Tony said. 'Once we're round the corner I'm gonna pull up. Drop your disposable on the kerb, switched on. Got it?'

'Got it!'

They turned into a side street and pulled up in the shadows and Marta did as she had been instructed. But before she had closed the door, Tony stamped on the accelerator, giving his passengers a sharp jolt. Michael reached across and grabbed Marta's arm.

'What the fuck, Tony!' Marta cried.

Tony laughed and no-one spoke again until, five minutes later, they joined the East Parks autostrip.

'Here's the address,' Tony said, slipping a small square of paper into the drawer. 'He's at home today; him and his wife are entertainin' a couple of local businessmen.'

Michael swiftly outreached Marta and picked up the paper.

'Commissioner Dunai,' he read aloud. '17 Galati Avenue, Olt.'

He looked past Steffi, her head on her chest, deep asleep.

'Why Dunai?'

'Because you kept saying how understanding he's been about the memorial service, how he's always supported Green City. And everyone knows he's one of the few politicians in Brussels with any integrity.'

Michael frowns.

'But Olt's over three hundred kilometres.'

'Well,' Marta said with a grim smile. 'At least the roads will be quiet. I reckon we'll be there in time for breakfast.'

'It's a small village,' Tony continued, 'and the house is heavily guarded. You'll have to call ahead and make sure you speak to the guy otherwise you won't get nowhere close.'

Michael was looking decidedly sceptical.

'How many times have you two met?' Marta asked.

'Four. Five, maybe.'

'Well, don't worry, we'll have time to go over your script on the drive up.'

Michael shook his head; this was unreal. His long-standing respect for the police had already been dashed. Now here he was, about to go calling on the Regional Commissioner with a claim that the man hunting the Union House bombers was a killer. When Sophie used to go on about the police looking after their own he had always shrugged his shoulders. Now the questions whirring round in his head would not stop. How many others were involved in this conspiracy? Who could they trust? With East Parks up ahead, lit up like a funfair, he had no answers. But he was certain of one thing: Marta was right; they must press on.

'Wake up, Steffi,' he said, gently shaking his daughter. 'We're nearly there.'

Steffi slowly opened her eyes and looked around, dismayed. She was still yawning and rubbing her eyes when the taxi pulled up in Best-T's deserted forecourt.

'Thanks for everything, Tony,' Marta said. 'I owe you big time.'

'Sure,' Tony said, rubbing the thumb and forefinger of his right hand together.

Marta opened the door.

'Michael'll settle up,' she said, before stepping out and motioning Steffi to follow.

Tony unlocked the boot so that the women could retrieve their backpacks then looked over his shoulder at Michael.

'That's four hundred, Mike. Cash.'

'What? That's ten times the going rate. I'll give you—'

Marta appeared at the door.

'For God's sake, it's what I agreed,' she hissed. 'Just pay him.'

Grumbling to himself, Michael pulled a wad of notes from his pocket, peeled off four hundreds and slipped them into the tray.

'Good luck,' Tony said, tucking the notes into the top pocket of his shirt. 'I'll be listening out.'

Michael gave a surly nod, slipped from the taxi and strode after Steffi and Marta. Relieving his daughter of her backpack, he shepherded her through into Best-T's reception. Marta, meanwhile, lingered by the soaring glass frontage to watch Tony head back down the drive. Once the taxi had turned out onto the road she crossed to the waiting area, where Steffi was slumped on a black leather settee, her eyes half-closed.

'Look, they've got a drinks machine,' she said brightly. 'And it's free. What would you like?'

'Cappuccino… Please,' Steffi groaned.

Marta sat her backpack beside the others' bags and crossed to the machine. While waiting she looked over at the desk where, judging by the sour look on the receptionist's face, Michael was not receiving a very warm welcome.

'There's a fifty in it for you and your colleague if you get it done in ten,' she heard him say with impressive authority.

The man's face lit up.

'We'll do our best, sir,' he said, picking up the phone.

Michael nodded curtly and came over to join Marta at the drinks dispenser.

'What was he beefing about?'

'He wasn't happy with our "unscheduled" appearance. Jobsworth.'

Marta shot Michael a broad grin.

'Looks like you're learning,' she said.

He laughed.

'I suppose you could say I'm adapting.'

Marta picked up the drinks and returned to the waiting area, where Steffi had nodded off once more. She sat down on the settee opposite, placed Steffi's coffee on the table between them and savoured her chocolate. After all the tension and dashing around of the last few hours, the warmth and stillness and barely audible muzak was so relaxing. How she craved just a moment's—

Michael sat down heavily beside her.

'I've been thinking about the route,' he murmured.

Yanked awake, Marta swallowed another mouthful of her drink.

'We can't use the R46; there are too many tollbooths and cameras. But the B-road to Bucharest passes close to Olt. The 504, I think.'

'Great. I'm happy to share the driving. At least that way we can both get some sleep.'

'Oh, yeah! And when was the last time you drove any car, let alone a manual?'

Marta shrugged.

'Manual, petrol, electric... They're all just cars.'

'Let's see what happens when we hit the road, eh? If everything's running...'

Steffi opened her eyes and let out a huge yawn before rolling over. Michael gazed affectionately at his daughter before turning back to Marta.

'I'm sorry you got dragged into this.'

'I could say the same. I'll always be grateful for what you did tonight.'

Michael gave her a bleak smile.

'I guess we're quits then.'

They sipped their drinks in silence. If the phone on reception hadn't buzzed, Marta would have been asleep in seconds.

'And what time will you be needing the vehicle, sir?' the receptionist asked in his smarmiest voice. 'And what about fuel? ... Fine. Your vehicle will be ready at zero six-forty. Thank you. Goodbye.'

Almost immediately, the telephone buzzed once more.

'OK, mate... Mr Brancusi, your vehicle's ready, sir.'

Michael got up, waved his acknowledgement and went over to his sleeping daughter.

'Wake up, Chickpea. Time to go.'

Steffi did not stir so Michael shook her shoulder firmly. This time she sat bolt upright and looked around, a dazed expression on her face.

'You can go back to sleep once we get in the car.'

Steffi's face clouded over as she realised her nightmare was no dream.

Once the acceptance forms had been signed and the promised fifty handed over, the trio picked up their bags and gathered by the front door. Seconds later the Merc slid down the ramp and pulled up beneath the forecourt lights. Michael stepped out into the cool, rousing air.

'I've filled her up, sir,' the attendant said. 'She's all ready to go.'

Michael thanked the lad and opened the boot, just as a black saloon screeched to a halt in the road, smoke billowing from its tyres. Everyone froze, shocked by the explosion of noise and movement, as the driver leaped from the vehicle and started up the driveway. Marta recognised the heavy, menacing movements straightaway, the bulk beneath that dark suit. It was Pal.

'Stay where you are,' the captain bellowed. 'You can't get away, the place is surrounded.'

Michael, his heart pounding, glanced over at Steffi, who was clinging to Marta's arm and looking absolutely petrified.

'Quick,' he yelled, throwing his backpack over his shoulder. 'Up the ramp.'

The two women did not need telling twice and, grabbing their bags, dashed across the forecourt and into the welcoming shade of the tunnel.

*

Sprinting up the circular ramp after Marta and Steffi, Michael expected to feel the hammer blow of lead burying itself in his back. But there were no shots, no further shouts, just the sound of his own desperate gasps and Pal's boots, fading the higher they went. By the time the fugitives had completed a half-dozen laps their pursuer's footsteps had completely died away. One floor further on and Michael found Steffi and Marta slumped against the wall, panting furiously, their backpacks on the ground.

'Keep going,' he called out. 'There's a bridge on the sixth.'

'I can't breathe,' Steffi cried.

'Come on,' Michael shouted, jogging slowly past his daughter. 'We need to keep moving.'

Marta pulled on her backpack and set off after Michael, looking around every few paces to make sure that Steffi was keeping up. Her heart pounding, her ribs aching, she recited to herself over and over: *We're gonna make it. We're gonna make it.*

They stopped just short of the entrance to the sixth floor, dropped their packs on the ground and gulped down the air. At length, when her pulse and breathing had steadied, Marta dug out a bottle of water from her satchel and took a long swig.

'Christ,' she whispered, handing the bottle to Steffi. 'I think I'll stick to the pool in future.'

Michael wiped his forehead on his sleeve and shook his head.

'I haven't had as much exercise since the army.'

Steffi, her mouth hanging open, slid down the wall to sit on the concrete and gulp greedily from the bottle.

'I'm just going to take a look,' Michael said, nodding towards the entrance. Steffi offered her father the bottle and he finished what was left before inching forward to the top of the ramp. Marta, shivering as the sweat on her neck and back cooled in the chill night air, told Steffi she was going to check behind them and crept down the ramp one level to listen out for any signs of movement. There were none and, barely two minutes later, she rejoined Steffi and her father.

'The top floor's lower than the first five,' Michael recalled. 'It's laid out like a regular park, single layer, no stacks. That means less cover, but if we crawl between the rows and keep low we should be able to stay out of sight of the cameras. And once we get to the walkway we can cross to the next block. It's twice the size of this one and we can find somewhere to hide away until things calm down. Are you ready?'

Steffi and Marta nodded and the three of them picked up their packs, tiptoed to the entrance and peered around the wall. Michael pointed to the walkway, just visible at the far end of the dimly lit space, beyond the rows of anonymous, dustsheet-covered shapes.

'Let's just go, Dad,' Steffi whispered. 'We could make it in one.'

'We need to be careful, love. The police will know about the bridge; they could be in there already, waiting for us. And then there're those...' He pointed at the CCTV cameras fixed to the ceiling. 'They're probably watching us right now.'

A minute or so later, when they were as sure as they could be that no-one was lying in wait for them, they crouch-ran to the nearest block of vehicles and hid between the first two rows. Kneeling on the dusty concrete, Marta wondered what was going on outside. Where was Pal? What he was he up to? And where were the regular police and the Parks' security people? They'd heard no sirens or voices, no 'copters or drones. For a building meant to be surrounded, apart from the distant hum and thump of the Park's industrial units, it was eerily quiet.

Michael turned to Marta.

'I'm going to check that the walkway's clear. Have you got your keys?'

Marta frowned, intrigued, but unzipped the backpack's outer pocket and produced her keyring.

'Great.'

Michael lifted the dustsheet of the vehicle they were kneeling beside to reveal a black hub retainer. He tapped it gently with his wedding ring to check that it was metal. It was.

'Keep your eye on the lift and tap hard three times if you see the light move. OK?'

Marta nodded and slipped the ring with its two worn keys onto her little finger.

'And you, Chickpea, can you crawl over there and keep your eye on the ramp, just in case?'

Steffi nodded wearily as reality and exhaustion kicked in once more. Michael leaned forward and planted a kiss on his daughter's forehead. She seized his hand.

'Be careful, Dad.'

'I'll be back before you know it,' he said, gently easing his hand from his daughter's grasp before climbing to his haunches and shuffling to the front edge of the row. Marta followed and crouched down behind him.

'It's down on one,' she said, eyeing the lift some thirty or so metres away. 'Take care.'

Michael nodded and prepared to make his run. But just as he was about to go he felt a tug on his jacket and turned to find Marta beaming fondly up at him. They kissed briefly and hugged each other before he turned and launched himself at the neighbouring row, dropping out of sight of the cameras the moment he reached the far side of the aisle. Marta turned to see Steffi looking at her, her brow furrowed.

'Well?' she whispered, shooing her away.

Steffi gave a faint smile then turned and crept swiftly to the front of the neighbouring row.

As most of the dustsheets reached the ground Marta had no clear view beneath the parked cars. But less than a minute later she spotted Michael bob up by the low wall at the edge of the facility. After checking that the lift was still on '1' she crept back to the middle of the row, where the vehicle's height provided better cover, and raised her head. Michael was still in the same spot, peering over the edge of the wall, presumably to see… *Sweet Jesus, the lift's on two!* Marta dropped to her knees and reached forward to tap furiously on the wheel. One. Two. Three. Her heart thumping, she shuffled further forwards. Michael was no longer visible. And the lift was on '4'.

'Marta?'

Marta spun round to see Steffi crawling towards her. The girl looked terrified.

'What's happening?'

'The lift's coming up,' Marta whispered urgently. 'Keep down and stay quiet.'

The lift bell pinged, the doors opened and out stepped Pal, alone, pistol in hand, the same mean look on his face that Marta had seen at the press conference on TV. Heading for the spot where Marta had last seen Michael, he kept his back to the wall and paused to inspect each gap, crouching down to scan any exposed areas. How deadly cool and practised he looks, thought Marta, the hunter stalking his prey. She felt her heart pounding against her ribs, her insides turn to jelly. *Think, woman, think.* Then, suddenly, everything made sense: the absence of any other cops, the abandoned chase…No cop would ever go out on a shout alone at night in Caradea; it was simply too dangerous. They weren't surrounded at all, she decided. Pal was acting on his own.

'Steffi Brancusi. I know you're here, show yourself. If you surrender now, I promise you'll come to no harm. The same goes for your father and Ms Ionescu.'

Marta looked round at Steffi, who was sitting with her back to the vehicle, her arms wrapped around her knees. The teenager, ghostly pale, gave her a woeful look and Marta knew she needed to act quickly. There was no way this madman was going to let any of them go free; this had all gone way beyond—

'Come on, Steffi,' Pal called out again, 'give yourself up. You'll be safe with me.'

Marta leaned back to stare up at the ceiling and shouted as loud as she could.

'PAL.'

The policeman leapt up and, as he frantically scanned the lines of shrouded vehicles, Michael launched himself at him. Pal hit the floor with an enormous grunt and Steffi lurched forward and wrapped her arms around Marta. A shot exploded in their ears and Steffi screamed and started shaking uncontrollably. Holding the girl tightly, Marta listened, horrified, as the struggle continued, shoes scuffing on the rough concrete, dull thumps and grunts ringing out as the two men collided with one vehicle after another.

And then their voices mingled in one final, diminishing chorus and came to an abrupt end with a muted thud.

Marta and Steffi lay on the floor, clinging to one another as they adjusted to the sudden silence, the return of the Parks' regular sounds. After what felt like an age, Marta gently disentangled herself from her weeping friend and crawled to the edge of the row. Peering above the car hood she could see no sign of either man, hear no sounds suggesting any movement. Had they gone over the edge? Was either of them still alive? Marta inspected the lift indicator, static on 6, then crept back and knelt down beside Steffi.

'Steffi... Steffi, listen to me,' she said, taking the girl's hand. 'I'm going over there to have a look. You stay—'

'Don't leave me,' Steffi cried, burying her face against Marta's thigh. 'I don't want to be left alone.'

Marta was afraid of what they might find but did not have the time to argue.

'OK, OK, we'll both go,' she said, grabbing her bag. 'Up you get.'

There did not seem to be any point in creeping about any more, trying to avoid the cameras; the dazed couple were done with running. They made their way slowly across the aisle and between the cars opposite, looking around anxiously as they went. But there was no tinging lift and no pounding feet and, when they emerged from the far row, no Michael or Pal, either. Only the cop's pistol lying on the ground and a few dishevelled dustsheets gave any clue that the struggle they had witnessed had actually taken place. Marta crossed to the wall, preparing herself for what she was certain she was about to discover. Steffi hung back, biting her lip. When Marta reached the wall and leaned over she saw the two lifeless bodies lying entwined on the floodlit grass. She studied Michael, his arched back and oddly twisted leg, his bloody face, looking for signs that he was still alive. It was hard to tell from this distance but, even if the cop had cushioned his fall, it was unlikely that either of them could have survived such a drop.

Reaching into her bag, Marta pulled out the disposable that Tony had given her, intending to dial 112. But just then Steffi appeared beside her and, although Marta told her not to look, the teenager insisted, thrusting her knuckles between her teeth when she saw what Marta had seen. Marta put her arm around the girl's shoulders and the two of them stood there, desolate.

'You just can't leave things alone, can you, Marta…?'

The women spun round to see Arpad standing behind them, his hands on his smart, tailored hips, his face wearing the same look of loathing that Marta had last seen at Adrian's place.

'…You just have to keep sticking your big ugly nose into other people's business.'

Seeing the look on Steffi's face, Arpad spat on the ground.

'Yes, beautiful, it's me again,' he sneered. 'Good job the cops came or we'd've done for you, too.'

Marta eyed the ragged scar that ran down Arpad's left cheek.

'Pretty, ain't it?' he said, marking the direction of her gaze. 'They gave me a good going-over, your friends. Should have seen the replay, though, Marta, I had 'em crying like little girls.'

Arpad stepped forward and grabbed a fistful of Steffi's hair and the teenager shrieked as he yanked her down.

'I promised my partner I'd fuck you before I—'

Marta leaped at Arpad's outstretched arm and buried her nails in his wrist. She heard the click of a swish-blade and, too late, felt the excruciating pain as he slashed the back of her hand in one brutal swipe. When he drew back the knife to renew his attack Marta stumbled away, her limp, injured hand hanging loose. Once out of reach, weeping with the pain, she fumbled frantically inside her bag with her one remaining hand. Steffi, meanwhile, freed from her attacker's grip, crawled desperately after her friend, screaming. But Arpad was on the girl in an instant, crouching over her and licking her ear as he placed the blade against her throat.

'Shame we haven't got time,' he said calmly. 'We could have had such a—'

Arpad yelped as Marta fell on him and thrust the StunMaster against his neck. As he rolled to the ground, his body convulsing, Steffi scrambled clear. But Marta was not done yet. Kicking the knife away, she dropped down by Arpad's side and continued her crazed attack, zapped him repeatedly, driving the crackling StunMaster into his face and crotch.

'What's up, sicko?' she screamed, the blood from her useless hand spattering his face and suit. 'Don't you like Mr Sparky tickling your bits? Here's one from Gypsy and here's—'

Suddenly the enraged Marta felt two powerful arms envelop her body and yank her roughly away from her victim, now shaking uncontrollably on the floor, piss staining his once-pristine suit. Slowly, very slowly, she felt her anger subside as cops appeared from everywhere, easing the StunMaster from her hand, helping Steffi to her feet, resuscitating the prostrate Arpad. Leaning back she looked up at the friendly face staring down at her.

'Jotti, what are you doing here?'

And then she fainted.

TWENTY-FIVE

With that single swipe, Arpad's sharp blade had caused extensive damage to the tendons and nerves of Marta's left hand and fractured two metacarpal bones. Post-operative complications requiring a return to theatre meant that her stay in hospital extended into a second week, causing her considerable frustration on top of the persistent pain. Far worse than all of that, though, was the lingering heartbreak that Michael's death had triggered. She had not realised the strength of her feelings for that brave, gentle soul and his bright and troubled – now doubly orphaned – daughter. As each interminable night dragged on she lay awake in her darkened side-room, reliving the adrenaline-soaked flight to East Parks and that final battle with Arpad before invariably dreaming of what might have been…

Fortunately, there were plenty of distractions during the day, from the nurses dispensing care and medication to the orderlies giving out meals and the doctors conducting ward rounds. The g-mails and messages from friends, work colleagues and well-wishers poured in, while Dina was a star, visiting every day before or after work, bringing in sweets and magazines and her own inimitable brand of gossip. Meanwhile, Flori looked after the youth club, opening and locking up the hall, managing the volunteers and supplying Marta with regular updates on the kids. She also took it upon herself to organise the annual outing, a week's outward bound near the coast.

'It was my suggestion in the first place,' she told Marta. 'It's only right that I should pick up the slack.'

On the evening of Marta's admission, soon after she had returned from theatre, Commander Litani had come to see her. He sat in the large easy chair by the head of the bed, one long leg crossed elegantly over the other, and paid tribute to her bravery. He was most solicitous, too, enquiring after her comfort and checking that she had everything she needed. He even apologised for the armed guard outside her room, explaining that he intended to take no risks with her safety. At length the true purpose of the policeman's visit became clear when he asked Marta if she felt up to talking about the previous night's events and everything leading up to them. When Marta said that would be OK the Commander had gone to the door and asked a detective colleague, waiting in the corridor, to join them. But Marta had misjudged just how exhausted she was and, in that warm and peaceful place, with the Commander's rich, deep voice running through the formalities – stressing that the purpose of the conversation was purely to assist with inquiries, seeking her confirmation that she willingly and without duress consented to participate – her heavy eyelids soon closed themselves. The next time she opened her eyes it was the middle of the night and the room was in darkness. She was alone. The two policemen returned the following day and got their statement, and again the day after that with further questions. But since then the only time she had seen the Commander was on TV, fronting the police press conferences that followed in the wake of Pal's death and exposure.

Despite Marta telling them that they shouldn't bother, her mother and Aunt Lisha visited the hospital a couple of times, too.

On both occasions Mrs Ionescu chided her for getting mixed up with 'scum' like Radics, insisting that she had known from the start he was a bad 'un. But having got the finger-wagging out of the way, the old woman revealed her concern for her daughter, her eyes filling up when she recounted how the police had arrived at the apartment early in the morning to inform her of Marta's hospitalisation, how she had prayed throughout the entire six and a half hours that Marta was in theatre the second time around. Aunt Lisha, meanwhile, had been following the news avidly and taken it upon herself to act as the official archivist of all items relating to what became known as the 'East Parks incident'. Of course, Marta was well able to keep abreast of developments via the pad that Dina had loaned her (the police having retained her devices for analysis). But she didn't like to appear ungrateful to her aunt, especially as she was clearly deriving so much pleasure from her new role, describing the revelations concerning Pal's corruption, and his and Radics's sex-smuggling conspiracy, with considerable relish. The pensioner had seemed positively gleeful when reporting that international arrest warrants had been issued for over twenty gang members. But not all the news was relayed with such gusto: reports of the execution of the two reception staff at Best-T, apparently carried out just minutes after Marta, Michael and Steffi had fled into the storage facility, were delivered with marked solemnity.

Despite these and Marta's other daytime distractions, the news headlines and police press conferences, there was one subject that was much dearer to her heart than any other: Steffi's progress and wellbeing. Marta remembered how she had felt after her father died of natural causes when she was in her early twenties. Quite what it must feel like to lose both parents at such a young age, prematurely and so close together, she could only guess. The two friends spoke or messaged one another once or twice every day after that fateful night at East Parks, but, much to Marta's consternation, Steffi seemed remote, their exchanges wooden and superficial. How was Marta's recovery progressing? What was the food like in hospital? When did she think she would be discharged? Any questions Marta asked about how Steffi was feeling and what she had been up to elicited only the most general responses. Her interviews with the police were 'boring'. Her grandparents had moved into Roman House and were handling her father's funeral arrangements. The Principal at her school had arranged a meeting to discuss her pastoral care. It was as though Steffi was distancing herself from the world, Marta thought, turning in on herself just as she had done after Petra was imprisoned.

All that changed on the sixth day of Marta's incarceration, when Steffi, having first called to make an 'appointment', came to visit, bringing with her a huge bouquet of flowers and a box of fancy chocolates. They embraced, stiffly, and Steffi sat back in the easy chair just out of reach. It took a while to re-establish contact, to provoke a real smile or a sarcastic response. But gradually Steffi started to thaw out and, at last, Marta felt able to ask what she had been wanting to ask since the teenager had walked into the room.

'So, how are you doing?'

Steffi sighed, only this time Marta detected a weariness of the soul rather than the incredible physical weariness and fear when she'd last heard the girl make that noise.

'To be honest, Marta, I'm a bit overwhelmed. Grannie and Grandad Brancusi are driving me mad. I mean, I appreciate their support but all the fussing's getting to me. And now Grandpa Bernhard and Grandma Gertrud have arrived from Munich and are staying at the Royal until the funeral.'

Marta nodded. She wanted to appear neutral, to let Steffi get out of her system whatever was troubling her. There it was again, that sigh.

'They've asked if they can meet you.'

'Who has?'

'Grandpa Bernhard and Grandma Gertrud.'

'Me? Why?'

'They want to thank you for... for everything.'

Steffi was starting to look very uncomfortable.

'And?'

'They want me to go and live with them in Munich.'

Marta recognised the stab of jealousy that Steffi's statement prompted. Knowingly or otherwise, her affections were being tested.

'So... How do you feel about that?'

'I don't want to go. I mean, they're lovely and we get on really well but... my school's here, my friends and... I want to be near to you.'

Marta's heart leapt. *So this is what it feels like...* She raised her arms and Steffi, tears in her eyes, jumped up and stepped into her welcoming embrace. Marta's splinted hand complained mightily but she didn't care; this moment was worth all the pain.

TWENTY-SIX

Marta stood in the kitchen, nudging the roses into position in a glass vase with the back of her gloved left hand. Jotti sat on the sofa, sipping his coffee and watching her, his jacket hanging over a chair, his shoulder holster on view. Behind him, storage crates and taped-up boxes littered the living area. The comscreen had been packed away.

'They're beautiful, Jotti. Thank you.'

'You're welcome.'

Marta carried the vase over to the living area and set it down on the dining table. She went back to the kitchen to collect her mug then returned and sat down in the easy chair.

'Coffee OK?'

'Great.'

Marta sipped her drink, not wanting to rush things.

'So, why you?' she asked at length.

Jotti pondered her question before replying.

'We knew Radics was using the Welcome Homes as a drop-off point for the women the gang smuggled in from Ukraine and Russia. And we knew the couriers who accompanied them. But we didn't know the rest: the gang members at the other end, what happened to the money the trafficked women and their families paid, and the bent cops this end who were in on it. So, the powers that be decided we needed someone on the inside, close to Radics. It had to be an unfamiliar face, someone with no connection to the local force.'

Marta nodded, appreciating Jotti's candour.

'And poor Ludmilla Fedoruk?'

Jotti shrugged.

'I guess if she hadn't broken ranks, she and Sophie Brancusi would still be alive and we'd still be searching for evidence.'

Silence.

'Any news on Enver?' Marta asked.

'No, nothing.'

She sighed and shook her head.

'God. I don't know how you can do your job.'

Jotti finished his coffee, stood up and reached for his jacket.

'Someone's got to. And it does have its perks.'

He pulled on his jacket, leant down and kissed Marta on the cheek. She smiled, put down her mug and got to her feet.

'Shame, really, you made a great barman.'

Hearing the sound of a key in the front door, Jotti shifted his gaze. The door opened and Steffi walked in wearing her winter school uniform. She gave Jotti a big smile.

'Marta said you were coming.'

The teenager dropped her backpack on the carpet and closed the door.

'You're looking well, Ms Brancusi.'

'Marta spoils me.'

Marta laughed.

'It'll all end tomorrow.'

Jotti frowned.

'Tomorrow?'

Marta waved at the crates and Jotti shook his head.

'Of course… Geez, your place was riddled,' he told Steffi. 'Took three sweeps to clean it up.'

'Well, I'm looking forward to seeing it again.'

Marta snorted.

'And I'm looking forward to having a housekeeper.'

Steffi laughed and put her arm around Marta's shoulders.

'Marta or Maria. Now who'll win that one, I wonder?'

Jotti grinned.

'Well, good luck. Both of you.'

Steffi opened the door. Jotti nodded to her and stepped out onto the walkway. Marta followed him out.

'If you're ever passing Petreni…'

'Sure, Princess.'

Marta watched Jotti disappear into the stairwell then stepped back inside and closed the door.

Steffi looked at her expectantly.

'Well? Did you file them?'

'File what?'

'The adoption papers, dummy.'

Marta lifted her hand to her mouth and Steffi stared at her, shocked.

'Don't tell me you forgot!'

Marta grinned.

'Gotcha!'

Steffi rolled her eyes and mock-swiped the top of Marta's head.

'*Dummkopf.*'

The two of them embraced happily.

TWENTY-SEVEN

Under the watchful gaze of Gyula Bokros, two burly men lifted a box from the tail of the removal van parked outside Roman House, crossed the pavement and entered the security vestibule. A people carrier pulled up behind the van and Marta hopped out and slid open the side door. Her mother shuffled forward and took Marta's hands. Tentatively, the old lady lowered first one foot and then the other onto the step then down onto the pavement. Looking up at the building's façade she scowled.

'Mother's apron, what an ugly old place!'

Steffi stepped down behind Marta's mother, handed the old lady her stick and offered her her arm. Mrs Ionescu took it.

Aunt Lisha leaned out of the van and waved away Marta's proferred hand.

'So it's back to Goval then, Ele?'

Mrs Ionescu sniffed.

'We'll see inside first.'

Steffi turned and grinned at Marta and her aunt.

'I'm sure you'll like it here, Mama,' she said.

'Huh,' Mrs Ionescu snorted. 'Don't count on it, girl.'

The four women headed slowly across the pavement and entered the building.

ABOUT THE AUTHOR

Anthony Etherington grew up in Coventry, attended Warwick University as a mature student and gained an honours degree in Management Sciences. Now retired and living in Kenilworth, he has written several short screenplays and teleplay pilots as well as three feature length dramas. One of these, Yellow Dragon and the Red Fox, won Best Screenplay awards at the European Independent Film Festival and The International Film Festival of Wales in 2014. Two of his short scripts – Flotsam and Gemma's War – have been filmed and are available to view on YouTube. Europia is his debut novel.